Coop saw the house first

In the fading sunlight it looked more than weathered. The clapboard was badly in need of paint and the barn appeared to be in even worse condition. He also saw that several head of cattle had strayed through a broken section of wire fencing.

He slammed on his brakes. In the distance he noticed a skinny woman, a blonde, who had a small child hanging on to her jacket, attempting to shoo the animals back.

"Hold on," Coop yelled after he set his brake and rolled down one window. "I'll come give you a hand."

The woman's head jerked around in surprise, as if she hadn't heard his engine and had no idea anyone was on the road.

Cooper swept up the straw cowboy hat he wore when working out in the sun and leaped down from the cab. He began turning the closest cattle back into the would-be enclosure.

At last the final stubborn rangy steer in the group of two dozen or so crossed over the squashed wire. Facing the woman, who stood closer to him now, Coop dragged his shirtsleeve across his brow. When he opened his eyes, shock traveled from his suddenly tight jaw straight to his toes.

Though a great deal thinner, and her sky-blue eyes far more lackluster than when he'd last seen her, the much-talked-about widow was none other than Cooper's first love, Willow Courtland. Willow, who'd married his arch enemy, Tate Walker.

Dear Reader,

I've often considered writing a story in which either the hero or heroine has a child with autism. I discovered how difficult such a story is to write. I have a grandson on the autism spectrum and I've learned that it's a disorder with so many variables it's impossible to fit them all into one fictional child.

The reality for the parent of an autistic child is that finding appropriate programs can be a problem—although there are more available now than there once were. Still, if you're from a rural area as my heroine is, the task can seem insurmountable. And if, like Willow, you're also trying to run a ranch and raise a child on your own, life is—to put it mildly—not easy.

That's why I searched for a hero like Cooper Drummond. A man who, while not without his faults, has a heart big enough to love a woman out of his past and her autistic child.

I hope you enjoy Willow, Lilybelle and Cooper's story. I love hearing from all my readers. You can contact me by email at rdfox@cox.net.

Or by letter at Roz Denny Fox, 7739 E. Broadway Blvd #101, Tucson, AZ 85710-3941.

Sincerely,

Roz

The Maverick Returns

Roz Denny Fox

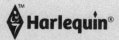

TORONTO NEW YORK LONDON
AMSTERDAM PARIS SYDNEY HAMBURG
STOCKHOLM ATHENS TOKYO MILAN MADRID
PRAGUE WARSAW BUDAPEST AUCKLAND

Recycling programs
for this product may
not exist in your area.

ISBN-13: 978-0-373-75408-3

THE MAVERICK RETURNS

This edition published by arrangement with Harlequin Books S.A.

For questions and comments about the quality of this book please contact us at Customer_eCare@Harlequin.ca

® and TM are trademarks of the publisher. Trademarks indicated with ® are registered in the United States Patent and Trademark Office, the Canadian Trade Marks Office and in other countries.

www.Harlequin.com

Printed in U.S.A.

ABOUT THE AUTHOR

Roz saw her first book, *Red Hot Pepper*, published by Harlequin Books in February 1990. She's written for several Harlequin series, as well as online serials and special projects. Besides being a writer, Roz has worked as a medical secretary and as an administrative assistant in both an elementary school and a community college. Part of her love for writing came from moving around with her husband during his tenure in the Marine Corps and as a telephone engineer. The richness of settings and the diversity of friendships she experienced continue to make their way into her stories. Roz enjoys corresponding with readers either via email, rdfox@cox.net, or by mail (7739 E. Broadway Blvd #101, Tucson, AZ 85710-3941). You can also check her website www.Korynna.com/RozFox.

Books by Roz Denny Fox

This book is for Paula Eykelhof, who has supported and encouraged me in my writing for as long as I've been dreaming up stories. Also Cooper and Willow's story is for Kathleen Scheibling, who found a place in American Romance for one more good-looking, lovable Texas cowboy.

Chapter One

It was Saturday night, and Cooper Drummond, five-time national bronc-riding champion, sat in a Hondo, Texas, bar, nursing his second beer. The barmaid flirted with him, as did rodeo fans who were trying to get his attention. They eventually gave up and turned to someone else when Coop didn't flirt back. He had a lot on his mind. It had begun to bother him that he had very little to show for five years of earning good money on the circuit. He owned a top-of-the-line Dodge Ram and a color-coordinated two-horse trailer. He had a suitcase full of flashy buckles, more than one man would ever wear. He'd lost count of his broken bones. Thank heaven they'd all healed. With luck he wouldn't have any more, now that—six months ago—he'd quit rodeo. He'd been working for Jud Rayburn on the Rocking R Ranch because he didn't want to go home to the Tripe D, which his older brother ran with an iron fist—just like he tried to run Coop's life. Tonight ought to be a typical Saturday night off from chasing rogue steers through dusty, cactus-littered arroyos. As a rule Coop would hit town with a group of other cowboys, and they all partied hard and two-stepped the night away with hangers-on from the rodeo days. But tonight, for some reason, his interest in dancing had disappeared. Some of his pals were playing pool in an adjacent room, but he wasn't moved to take part in that either.

On the jukebox, Reba belted out a song called "The Bridge You Burn." Her words, wrapped in upbeat music, bounced off the rafters and left Coop thinking about how many bridges *he'd* burned. A lot of them, for sure.

A hand clamped down on his shoulder, interrupting Coop's self-analysis. He turned on the bar stool, expecting to see one of the guys from the Rocking R. He didn't expect to see his older brother, Sullivan. Nor was Coop in any mood to have Sully pull out the adjacent stool and plant his butt there. The brothers had been at odds over almost everything since their dad died and Sully had nominated himself to fill his shoes.

Coop lifted his long-neck bottle and took a deep draw. "What brings you slumming tonight, big brother?"

"You. Why in hell are you working for the Rocking R instead of at home on the Triple D where you belong?"

"It hasn't been the *Triple* D since Dad died," Coop shot back. "You've made it the Single D."

"You want the brand changed to the Double D? It hasn't been double anything since you took off to prove something—hell if I know what. You rode every ornery bronc in the southwest when you could've raised the most profitable herd of quarter horses in Texas. You thought being a rodeo bum was better than doing everyday ranch chores, yet you're working for Jud like a common drifter."

"I sold my stock except for two geldings, and two

geldings don't make for good breeding, now do they? And Jud Rayburn treats me like a man—like I have a brain. He doesn't play lord and master like you do. But I'm leaving Jud's place and heading south. I read about a rancher advertising for a horse trainer down there."

"Really? Well, that makes this easier." Coop's brother pulled a sheaf of papers from the inside pocket of his corduroy jacket. "I've run the ranch alone for five years. I want you to sign Dad's third of the ranch over to my son, Gray." He unfolded the legal document and produced a gold pen that he held out to Cooper.

"Do you think this will force me to come back? Forget it! Gray's only six years old!" Coop set down his beer with a thwack.

"You were ten and I was fifteen when Mom died and Dad deeded us each a third of Drummond Ranch and renamed it the Triple D."

"Then we got equal parts of Dad's share when he died. So what?"

"After you graduated from college and got a hare-brained notion to run off to the rodeo, I've pulled your share of the workload, along with Dad's and mine."

"That's why I went off to rodeo, Sully. You put yourself in Dad's boots. I didn't like you ordering me around then, and I don't need it now." Coop grabbed the papers, ripped them in half and let the pieces drift to floor. Then, in a fit of long-brewing frustration, he hauled back and socked his brother in the jaw. Jamming on his hat, Coop stalked out, stiff-arming his way through the swinging door. He leaped into his pickup and roared out of the parking space without glancing back.

SULLY EXITED THE BAR, wiggling his jaw. His flinty gaze swept the area before his angry eyes fell on his pretty, red-haired wife, who waited for him near their car. She touched his face lightly and murmured, "Ouch. I can see that didn't go well. Shall we hike over to the diner and get some ice for your jaw, Sullivan?"

"I'm through with him, Blythe. He tore up the contract. I know, I know, you warned me against coming here. But I'm done, I tell you. Coop can't be a silent partner in the Triple D forever. I'm going to see our lawyer about voiding Coop's entire inheritance."

"Don't, Sully." Blythe gripped his arm. "Coop is family, and we have too little family left between us," she said, her eyes filled with sorrow. "Give it more time, then try again. Coop's young. He took your dad's death really hard. You know he thought Matt hung the stars and the moon." She sounded earnest. "Business at my clinic has picked up. You said stock sales were up, too. We're okay. Please, Sully. He's your only sibling, and Gray's only uncle. Please give Coop time to come around."

Sullivan, who'd loved Blythe since the day he met her in college, gave his jaw a last test before he sighed and kissed her. "Coop's not all that young. He's twenty-seven. Past time he grew up. What he needs is a good woman," Sully grumbled. "Yeah, he took Dad's death hard, but it's the way Willow Courtland dumped him that sent him off in a huff. She could've stopped him."

Blythe Drummond shook her head. "I don't suppose we'll ever know what really caused their breakup. Coop might have gotten over it if she hadn't married Tate Walker. That was like pouring salt in an open wound."

Sully yanked open the passenger car door and waited for Blythe to get in. "Yeah, but I say good riddance to Tate *and* to her. I wish Bart Walker would sell his ranch and leave. I can't prove he cut out some of my newborn calves and branded them with the Bar W, but I know there was bad blood between Dad and him over calf-rustling. All the Walkers are shady, to say the least."

Blythe swung her legs into the car. "Sully, you work too hard. And you worry too much about the Triple D, and about Cooper." She raised one hand. "No, no tirade. I don't care how much you gripe, I know you want Coop to come home. Why not hire someone to help you part-time for a few months? Coop's left the circuit for good. Give him until the holidays to work this out. Have you ever met a cowboy who doesn't get homesick at Christmas? If Coop doesn't wander home by then, we'll hunt him up and extend one last olive branch. Okay?" She smoothed a hand down Sully's rigid arm.

He blew out a breath. "If Coop comes home, we'll see if I feel inclined to give him a pass for the way he hit me. He had no call. And if I extend any olive branch, he'll have to show up at the Triple D to collect it."

STEAMED THAT SULLY had shown up at the bar unexpectedly, adding to his already disgruntled mood, Coop weighed his options on the drive back to the Rocking R. He had some money left from what he'd earned working for Jud. And some savings from when he sold the herd he'd built up before attending Texas A&M.

It was while he was in college that he'd developed a hankering to rodeo. But if his dad hadn't keeled over from a heart attack, and if Sully, who was five years older, hadn't taken it upon himself to run everything on the ranch, including him, things might have panned out differently. Maybe he wouldn't have fought with Willow. But then again… Ah, hell! Coop jammed in a CD and cranked up the sound. He hadn't thought about Willow in weeks. It didn't help now that Lady Antebellum filled the cab with "Need You Now."

He popped the disk out midsong and shoved in another that was better suited to his current mood. George Strait singing "All My Exes Live In Texas."

Coop didn't have any idea if Willow still lived in Texas. All ties were cut when she'd married Tate-the-jerk-Walker. His friends—and enemies—knew better than to mention either of their names to Coop. But it still hurt that she'd married that blowhard over him. They'd both vied for her attention from the day Willow's folks moved to Hondo when she was in the sixth grade. She knew how tough his dad's death had been on him. And she knew he hated the way Sully took charge of the ranch and ordered him around. Still, she'd chose that bad time to give him an ultimatum. Rodeo or her.

Drumming his fingers on the steering wheel, Coop felt the old gnawing emptiness well up again. Yes, her dad had been left wheelchair-bound from bull-riding. But she wouldn't listen when Coop explained that bull-riding was far more dangerous than busting broncs, something he'd done for easily half his life.

The song ended and George started crooning a mellower tune.

All of that was ancient history. Sully had already settled down, happily marrying Blythe Thompson, who'd become a veterinarian. Now they had a son. Coop hated to think that part of his attitude toward Sully was jealousy. But he would've married Willow, and they would've had a kid or two by now. Crap, he never should've come back to Hondo. It would be best if he packed up and left tonight, he decided. Like he told Sully, he had other options.

Coop had made up his mind by the time he reached the Rocking R. He went looking for Jud Rayburn. "Your roundup's winding down, Jud. I've decided to mosey down south. According to an ad in the newest *Horse Trader,* there's a rancher down near Laredo who is looking for a horse trainer. Everyone knows I'd rather work with horses than with cattle."

"I hate to lose you, Coop. Rest assured I'll give you a great reference. But surely you aren't leaving Hondo for good? I know Sully hopes you'll return to the Triple D."

Coop shook his head. "I doubt Sully still feels that way, Jud. He and I just had a run-in at Homer's bar." Coop flexed his right hand. "Sully's got a rock-hard jaw and I guess you could say I have an equally hard head. This wasn't our first argument."

"That's too bad, son. Matt would've wanted you boys to share the running of a ranch he loved. When your mom died, and Matt had to bury her, you and Sully were all that kept him sane. Kept him working and building up the ranch so that one day you boys would raise your families on the Triple D."

Swallowing a hard lump that came into his throat,

Coop said, "Yeah, well, that's working out for Sullivan and Blythe. Me, I'm not ready to let one woman tie me down."

Jud Rayburn cocked a shaggy eyebrow as he peeled off several twenties from a money clip and handed the bills to Coop. "There's a lot to be said for crawling into bed with the same woman every night, son. A woman who knows your weaknesses, but who only sees your strengths. When you land in Laredo, phone me with your address so if I haven't paid you enough, I can send you a check after the Rocking R accountant tallies your time sheets."

"This more than makes us square, Jud. Anyway, I don't want to make it easy for Sully to run me to ground." Coop shook hands with the rancher who'd been his dad's best friend. Crossing to the corral, he cut his two cow ponies out of the remuda, loaded them into his trailer and left.

Coop drove until midnight, then booked into a motel outside Laredo. He didn't sleep well. He was plagued all night by dreams of losing his mom when he was ten, then repeating the loss with his dad when he was in college. Coop had idolized Matthew Drummond. Tossing and turning, he punched his pillow into a ball. He wasn't ready or willing to admit how much like their father Sully had become. A quiet solid man's man. A good husband and dad, by all accounts. A hard worker. A pillar of the community.

Throwing back the covers, Coop hit the shower. He'd squandered too much of his rodeo earnings on a truck, and on beer and women. Coop let the water sluice over his body until it ran cold. He was sure his dad wouldn't be any happier with him at the moment than Sully was. Matt Drummond had been a peacemaker. Not liking the direction of his thoughts, Coop slapped off the faucets, dried quickly and dressed.

The late-June sky was streaked purple, red and orange when he threw his duffel bag into the pickup's cab and made his way out of Laredo to the McHenry spread. Summer heat would soon shimmer off the asphalt highway.

Bob McHenry was a big, bald, tobacco-chewing guy, who spat twice before telling Cooper he was darned sorry, but he'd already hired a horse trainer.

Coop thanked him and returned to his pickup after asking if he could water his horses at Bob's nearby trough. The whole spread was a nice, well-kept ranch, staked out by white tri-rail fences. Coop was disappointed he'd shown up too late. He would've liked working here, he thought.

"Hey, champ." A gnarled cowboy with a booming voice called out as Cooper watered his horses. He glanced around and spotted a bowlegged man pulling off his gloves after he climbed over the fence.

"Bob McHenry gave me permission," Coop said, thinking the cowboy was worried that he was up to no good.

Instead, the guy stuck out a hand. "Rafer James. You rode against my brother Lowell twice at the Mesquite rodeo. Beat him by seconds both times."

"Sure, I know Lowell. How is he? I quit the circuit myself after last season, but I don't recall seeing Lowell at the finals."

"He met a gal from Montana, got married and then

drew a bad hoss in an off-circuit rodeo. Crushed his hip against the chute. It never healed right. His wife wanted him to give up rodeoing, anyway. Her dad retired, so they took over running his feed store up near Bozeman."

Coop pursed his lips as Rafer asked him what he was doing in Laredo. "I saw the ad Bob placed for a horse trainer. He said he already hired someone, so I'll get on up the road and see if anyone needs a hand for summer haying, or maybe moving cows to a summer range."

The other man stuffed a stick of chewing gum in his mouth. "Things are tight in this part of the country, what with the bad economy and all. I've heard of a widow with a little kid, a daughter, who lives outside Carrizo Springs. She can't afford to pay scale, so she doesn't keep a hand for long. Seems she's barely hanging on since her husband died in a drunken brawl that ended in gunplay. Something else. The guys say she's a looker." The man nudged Coop's arm. "Up to now she's sent away any cowboy with ideas of getting into her bed. But, Champ, with your reputation on the circuit attracting buckle bunnies, I'll bet you can score. Unless the low wage drives you off."

Not sure he liked that picture of himself, Coop gathered his horses. "Isn't helping women in distress the unwritten code of the west?" he snapped.

"Whoa, there. I guess you think all those wins puts you up on a pedestal. I meant no offense to the widow. I'm only passing along rumors. Take the tip or leave it, I gotta get back to seeding a field."

The cowboy hobbled off. Deep down his jab reminded Coop too much of Sully's accusations, which made it rankle all the more. Perhaps guys like Rafer thought it was cool to have rodeo groupies always hanging around. It wasn't all that great. Coop liked women, and had no doubt taken advantage of some who were available on the circuit. But the past couple of years that lifestyle had gotten old.

Which was one reason Coop didn't immediately strike out for Carrizo Springs. Meandering in that direction, because it was how the single-lane highway ran, he stopped at every ranch he passed to see if anyone was hiring.

At two of those places the owners also mentioned the widow. Coop wasn't sure he wanted to get tangled up with a needy woman. He liked women who were successful in their own right.

One other thing about the network of drifter cowboys, news traveled quickly and efficiently. At a ranch near Artesia Wells, a ranch hand who'd recently been looking for work along the I-35 corridor told Coop the Triple D up near Hondo wanted to hire a part-time ranch manager. Just from now until Christmas.

Coop felt guilty. Not enough to backtrack and go home, but enough to take a more direct route to Carrizo Springs. The widow remained his ace in the hole, so to speak.

Then, luckily, he was able to hire on temporarily at a ranch outside Asherton. For three days he helped with branding, filling in for a cowboy who'd sprained his rope-throwing wrist. Branding was a hot, dirty, smelly business, but it earned Cooper some ready cash and a chance to shoot the breeze each evening with like-minded men, although most of this crew were Hispanic and only a few spoke English. The plus was that none of them seemed to have heard of Coop's rodeo achievements. Or if they had, they didn't put it together with the scruffy drifter who'd landed in their midst. And they sure didn't connect him to the well-known Triple D Ranch.

The first night after Coop had taken his turn in the shower and shaved, the youngest crew member joked that Coop looked too pretty to throw steers out of a chute and hold them down for branding. Coop just laughed. An older man, Alonzo, took out a harmonica as they sat watching the sun set, so Coop went to his pickup and got a guitar he used to play on the circuit to ease his nerves. For two evenings all the guys enjoyed playing universally popular tunes often used to quiet restless herds being driven to market. At the close of day three, Coop's tenure on this ranch ended. He felt bad saying adios to his new friends. Also, he didn't like this way of grabbing a few days of work here and there. He'd prefer a steady job.

Several miles out of Carrizo Springs he pulled into a lay-by and sat there for the longest time, reconsidering whether or not to go home—supposing home was still the Triple D. He needed to decide if he wanted it to be.

It was nine miles to Carrizo Springs according to his GPS. He could drive straight through the town, and take highway 83 to Uvalde. Then at the junction it would be a straight shot to Hondo and back to the Triple D. Jud Rayburn had told him that the house where he'd grown up sat empty. Sully and Blythe had built a new home on the vast acreage, nearer to Blythe's clinic.

Continuing to waffle about whether he was ready to let Sully become his boss, Coop left the lay-by. He stopped in Carrizo Springs for fuel, and for a bite to eat at a barbecue restaurant whose good smell enticed him from the gas station. It was a homey place, where the older waitress was friendly. She quickly spotted Coop for a stranger in town.

In the course of serving up mouthwatering ribs, she wormed out of him that he was an out-of-work cowboy. The waitress—Janey, according to her uniform tag—refilled the cola Coop drained. "Kinda close to summer for spreads around here to be hiring," she said. "But there's a woman ranch owner near here who's down on her luck. She has a young child. She could use a jack-of-all-trades." Janey looked Coop over. "I guess you've got enough muscle, and calluses on your hands, to fit that bill. That is, if you don't have monkey business on your mind."

"Monkey business, how?" Coop asked, as if he didn't know what she meant.

"She doesn't put up with any hanky-panky."

"Gotcha," Coop responded, but he rolled his eyes as he bit into a fat, juicy rib. He polished off his meal, paid the check and left Janey a good tip. At his pickup, he decided there was still enough daylight to take a run past the no-hanky-panky widow's ranch. Just for a look-see, he told himself.

Her ranch wasn't large enough to have a name, but Janey had provided decent directions. Coop saw the house first. In the fading sunlight it looked more than weathered. The clapboard was in need of paint. The porch ran downhill. Coop guessed a section under one end had rotted out. The barn appeared to be in even worse condition if that was possible. Round water troughs, half-buried in the ground, lacked water. Thirsty cattle milled around.

Coop slammed on his brakes. Several head of cattle had strayed through a broken section of wire fencing. In the distance he saw a skinny woman—a blonde, he thought—who had a small child hanging on to her jacket, attempting to shoo the animals back into the now-open enclosure.

"Hold on," Coop yelled after he set his brake and rolled down one window. "I'll come give you a hand."

The woman's head jerked around in surprise, as if she hadn't heard his engine and had no idea anyone was on the road.

Cooper swept up the straw cowboy hat he wore when working out in the sun, and leaped down from the cab. He began turning the closest cattle back into the would-be enclosure.

The two of them eventually made headway. She from one side of the road, he from the other. At last the final stubborn steer in the group of maybe two dozen crossed over the squashed wire. Facing the woman, who stood closer to him now, Coop dragged his shirt-sleeve across his brow to blot sweat he'd worked up. When he opened his eyes and took in the slender woman who'd yanked off her hat to fan her face, shock traveled from his suddenly tight jaw straight to his toes.

Though a great deal thinner, and her sky-blue eyes far more lackluster than when he'd last seen her, the much-talked-about widow was none other than Cooper's first love, Willow Courtland. Willow, who'd married his archenemy. Well, maybe calling Tate Walker his *archenemy* went a little far. But it had certainly been no secret around Hondo that Coop and Tate were bitter rivals. In school. In sports. And most assuredly for the affections of the woman staring at him now with total, abject shock on her face. Shock that mirrored the gut-twisting impact Cooper felt. Mouth dry, he couldn't speak.

Chapter Two

Willow Walker tried to blink away her shock. Tried to blink away what surely had to be an illusion. Thoughts of Cooper Drummond had filled her head so often since he went off to rodeo, she'd undergone a flash of hope, soon coupled with disbelief, and yes— vulnerability. She didn't want him to see her like this. Stringy hair. Grubby from chasing stupid steers. Down on her luck. Was she really close enough to reach out and touch the man she'd loved for more than half her life, the man she'd sent away and sworn to give up?

Neither of them spoke a word, adding to the surreal atmosphere. Willow couldn't have made a comment now if her life depended on it. There was a lump the size of Texas stuck in her throat. Suddenly she felt a tug on her limp hand, and Willow glanced down, cupping a sweaty palm reassuringly around her daughter's curly hair.

Tension continued to sing through the air as the cattle lowed and jostled one another for a spot circling the nearly empty, buried water barrel. Coop walked over to inspect it, and hung his hat on one of the surviving fence posts. Good sense screamed at him to hop back in his pickup and drive on down the road, code of the west be damned. He couldn't help the anger bubbling up inside him. He had five years of needing to vent his spleen at Willow bottled up.

Standing stiffly, allowing his gaze to slide over her from head to toe, what slammed Cooper in the chest was seeing her so thin, with an ever-growing wariness in dull blue eyes that used to sparkle all the time.

Something else tugged at his conscience. The skittish child hiding behind Willow. *Tate Walker's kid.* Coop's stomach tumbled and spun. He found it harder to swallow. He gritted his teeth to hold on to the old memories that told how long he'd nursed a broken heart thanks to this woman. The longer he stood silently clenching and unclenching his hands, the more Coop realized that his feelings for Willow weren't as dead as he'd like them to be. His earlier assessment of her home, her barn, her ranch and her appearance left him with a sharp concern for her well-being—a nagging worry about her immediate predicament. *She was a widow.*

Finding his voice, he said in a rush, "Look, I heard via the grapevine that you're in a bind here and could use some help. I didn't know it was you, Willow. But for old times' sake, I can lend a hand for a few days."

Choking on her embarrassment—because in the back of her mind Willow thought Coop had come in search of her—she managed to shake her head. The love she'd once had for Cooper Drummond fled, to be replaced by panic. He shouldn't be here. She didn't want him witnessing the depths to which she'd sunk. Scraping back her hair, she finally stammered, "I'm fine. I don't know why anyone would say I need help.

I'm fine. Fine," she reiterated more loudly, but dropped her hand to hide its shaking. "What are you doing here, anyway, Cooper? Why aren't you off at some rodeo?"

Her questions battered his unsteady senses. Willow was nowhere near as receptive to his offer as she ought to be, given the state of her ranch.

Avoiding eye contact with him, she scooped up her daughter and backed away.

The move gave Coop a clearer look at the child, age three or so, he'd guess. A small-boned, delicate, brown-haired girl with huge hazel eyes. In spite of her darker coloring, Cooper saw more of a young Willow in her daughter than he saw of his old nemesis, Tate Walker. But Tate was represented, too, in those hazel eyes.

Wilting under his scrutiny, Willow backed up farther.

Coop noticed right away how nervous she seemed, as if she was afraid of him. That made him reel. Surely Willow couldn't think he'd ever hurt her or any kid! Or that he'd held a grudge because of the callous way she dumped him. Still, Coop had to glance off into the distance to relax the tension cramping his jaw.

Once he felt at ease, he returned to her questions. "Willow, I've got eyes. Even if I hadn't heard at ranches along the route that you could use an all-around hand, this broken fence is plainly in need of muscle." He managed a halfhearted smile and playfully flexed an arm. Pride kept him from admitting that he'd left the rodeo. After all, their whole blow-up had been centered around his need to prove he could win big riding broncs, and her displeasure with that. "I'm just passing through," he said. "But I can spare some time to help you catch up on a few chores around this place."

"Just passing through on your way to the next rodeo?" she retorted.

With his fingers curling into his thighs, Cooper debated continuing to withhold information about his personal life that was really none of her business.

But what the hell, he decided in the next breath. A lot of years had rolled by since their split. "I guess you could say I got smart. I sure got tired of being dumped on my butt. The rodeo's out of my system. For the past six months or so, I've hired on to work at various ranches. Chasing strays. Branding. Helping with roundup." He raised one shoulder negligently.

A small frown appeared on Willow's face. "Pardon me for sounding nosy, but why are you signing on with various ranches? Why aren't you home working at the Triple D?"

Shifting away from her cool eyes, which pinned him down and made him flush guiltily, Coop grabbed his hat and settled it firmly on his head. Jiggling the post to see how solid it was, he blew out a sigh. "You probably don't know, since you moved away from Hondo, but Sullivan and I had a falling-out. You could call it a major disagreement. Many of them."

"Hmm. I see. That explains why you got this far down south, I suppose. However, none of it changes the fact that I really can't afford your services, Cooper." Now Willow drew in a huge breath and let it out in a heavy sigh.

"How do you fill your water barrels?" he asked. "You've got a passel of thirsty cows."

"I used to fill this one with a hose, but it split in a few spots, and most of the water leaks out between here and the well house. There's a pond on the property. I try to drive the cattle there twice a day. The silly things prefer to bolt through the fence to get to the stream across the road and down the hill. I'm lucky it's not a well-traveled highway."

"Maybe I can repair the hose temporarily with duct tape. I have a roll in my pickup. Unless you have couplings in the barn, the type to splice a hose."

She shook her head. "Don't trouble yourself. I tried duct tape, but the hose split in other spots. The sun will set soon, Coop. I'm not sure where you're heading next, but there are a number of fair-size cattle spreads up around Crystal City. You might find work that pays decent wages."

"Let's not discuss money. I can afford to donate a few days to an old friend."

Rallying momentarily, Willow grimaced and said, "Careful who you're calling *old,* Cooper Drummond. I'm a whole year younger than you, remember?" She expected him to laugh, but he studied her acutely and remained sober.

"I must look a sight," she mumbled, pausing to bury her blushing face in her silent daughter's shoulder. "I… It's getting late. I've been outside working all day."

"You look tired," Coop said diplomatically, really thinking she seemed tense and frazzled.

Willow flung out a hand. "Obviously you heard about Tate's death on your travels. This ranch isn't big by any stretch of the imagination. But I can't seem to keep up with everything that needs doing. Six months ago I decided to sell and listed with a Realtor in town. There's only been one lookie-loo and no takers. I haven't actually done a detailed count of my herd, but I believe I own about two hundred Angus steers. If I can figure out how to get them to market, that'll cut my workload a lot."

Coop surveyed the milling cattle. "You need to fatten them up if you hope to make any money off them at summer market. It's time to start adding corn to the grass they're still finding to graze on." He purposely didn't remark on her husband's death. Still, Willow's eyes seemed a bit vague to Cooper.

Bending, he reset a couple of metal posts the steers had pushed down. He jammed the tips into the soil with nothing more than brute force, then manhandled the wire fencing back on to hooks that lined the posts. Breathing hard, he said, "That'll only hold until the next adventurous cow bumps against it." He waved toward his color-coordinated truck and trailer. "I'm hauling two of my cutting horses. Why don't I saddle and bridle one, and drive these escape artists over to your pond? After that I can figure out what else is a priority around here."

She was quiet for so long, Coop spun back around to see Willow frown before she jerked her chin a couple of times in a reluctant nod.

"The pond's about a quarter of a mile straight back and up over a hill behind the barn," she said warily, as if she distrusted his real reason for making the offer.

Baffled by her hesitation, Coop eventually realized he could probably blame Tate's dislike of him for her wariness. After all, Tate had five years to fill her head with lies about him. Cooper felt a stab of sadness for what might have been. A stab of sadness for what he'd let go. He fought against a deeper ache, because while everyone up in the valley knew there never was any love lost between him and Tate, they all knew how both of them had fallen head over heels for Willow Courtland. She had no reason to ever doubt the trueness of a heart Coop always wore on his sleeve. But she'd unwittingly played into his and Tate's battle from junior high until after they'd gone to college at Texas A&M.

Instead of saying anything more, Coop backed his surefooted quarter horse Legend out of the trailer, then retrieved the sorrel he called Rusty. He led Rusty to a shade tree surrounded by patchy grass and looped his lead rope over a branch. About to comment on how cool it was beneath the old oak, Coop was surprised to discover that Willow had left and returned to the house. The screen door still quivered behind her.

He shook his head to clear it of memories reaching back to college days, when he and Willow had first made love, and then forward to the time he assumed he'd won the rivalry with Tate. It still galled him to think how easily Tate had stepped into his place when he'd taken off to rodeo. Tate had lost no time filling the void of Coop's absence, and as a result, Tate had walked away with the top prize. She was the woman Cooper had fully expected to spend his life with—the woman he'd expected to have his children.

That kind of reminiscing held only negative implications and no positives. Jaw locked, he tossed a well-worn saddle on Legend, slid on a bridle and climbed aboard the horse. Coop swept off his hat and with a satisfying cowboy yell of "Hiya hi hi!" he sent Willow's renegade steers trotting off in the direction of the pond.

WILLOW STOOD BY the living-room window, careful to stay in the shadows where Coop couldn't possibly see her, and admired the efficiency with which he rounded up and drove the cattle out of her front yard. She should've kept the horse that Tate's dad had given him when they moved to this ranch. But in the year since Tate's death, she'd had to let go of several items and animals, whose sale became necessary for their daily survival. Her daughter, Lillybelle, needed expensive care that wasn't readily available here.

Would it be so horrible if she accepted Cooper's offer to help out with some of the harder chores around the ranch? So what if he learned how big a mess Tate had left her in? Darn, but she tried so hard to keep up, to hold her head high, and not let on how dire her straits were. It shocked her when Cooper said folks had gossiped about her. She couldn't tell if he already knew Tate had died when she brought it up. Of course, the part-timers she'd hired probably had talked about her after they left. She'd backed a few of them off with an old unloaded shotgun, which she hated, although it served its purpose—deterring amorous cowboys on the prowl. Heaven only knew what hairy stories they told about her around the campfire. Some of the cowboys hadn't wanted to take no for an answer.

And therein lay the problem with letting Cooper Drummond stay a few days. The concern might not come from him—he'd always been a gentleman. It would more likely come from her, and the risk that she'd reveal how often he'd wormed his way into her thoughts over the years. Perhaps because of that, Willow had mistakenly assumed he'd come to find her. But why would he?

If she did let him handle a few chores, the same rules that she set for all her hired help would have to apply to him, as well. No fraternization with the lady of the ranch. Zero. Nada. Zippo. Even as she voiced the words aloud, her heart gave a little jolt, and she tried to ward off memories of how comforted she'd always felt in Coop's strong arms. As a boy who grew up tossing around hay bales and wrestling down steers for branding, he'd always had muscles. But now that he was a man, Willow could only imagine how years of keeping thousand-pound-plus bucking horses in check had honed Coop's upper body.

Shuddering, she thrust aside that particular image.

She led Lily to the kitchen table, and boosted her up on a wooden box tied to a chair. Willow retrieved a box of graham crackers, relishing the flash of delight in her child's eyes. She was less happy to see that the box was almost empty. So were her other cupboards, and her bank balance was severely strained. If Coop decided to stick around, he'd need to be fed. Working men, as she knew from having fed a few ranch hands of late, expected hearty meals. She scrimped, but she couldn't cut back when it came to feeding her daughter or the workers. She'd come to resent the way Tate had spent so much money on booze, gambling and women in town. He'd stopped working on the ranch, and as a result, he'd gone to flab. She'd have left if he hadn't sworn he'd have Lily taken away from her. That had scared her into staying.

Coop's arrival brought to the fore so many regrets that Willow had repeatedly told herself should remain buried with Tate. As her mother had pointed out, she'd made the choice to marry him. Made her bed, so to speak, and now needed to tough it out. Lie in it and cry in it, alone all her livelong nights.

OUT ON THE RANGE, Coop rode along the flimsy fence and noted several spots in need of reinforcement. There were two fields that should be ripe with summer hay, but which had been trampled by a herd that was probably too big for the acres Willow had.

Climbing off Legend, he inspected some winter grass chewed down to the roots. It was a field where summer rye should have been reseeded. Straightening, Coop squinted into the sun as he let a handful of soil filter through his fingers and watched it blow off in the wind. He tried to gauge if Willow had the resources to save her herd long enough to fatten them up and truck them to the nearest stockyard. Maybe yes. Maybe no.

All the ranchers he'd visited in the south of Texas had complained about the extended drought. Perhaps Willow figured it was a waste money to replant fields that might not produce. Except she had the pond. Near as Coop could tell, it was partially fed by the stream she'd mentioned, but there also had to be underground artesian springs for the pond to be so full of sweet water—a lifeline for the cattle she did have.

The whole place seemed awfully run-down considering that Tate had only died a year ago. On the other hand, who was he to judge? Coop chided himself. He had let Sully struggle alone to keep the Triple D afloat. Willow was alone too—and she had a child.

If coming here and stumbling upon her again did nothing else, it made Coop realize that when he finished helping Willow, it was time he go home. How far in the future that would be depended on how much assistance Willow was willing to let him provide.

She'd posted the ranch for sale. She probably didn't want to sink too much money into a ranch she didn't intend to hang on to. Even a small investment would increase her chances for attracting a buyer, but it'd been patently obvious that money was an issue with her. Unless her problem was with hiring him. Coop had to accept that Willow may not have harbored the same warm feelings he'd recently rediscovered. Feelings that, for him, had lain dormant. They'd had some good times back in the old days, he thought. Well, not *that* old, as Willow had pointed out. So, her humorous side wasn't totally gone.

WILLOW NEEDED TO clean Lilybelle after the graham crackers ended up all over her face and shirt. "Come on, girly. Shower time for us."

She took a few extra minutes to wash and blow-dry her own hair, all the while insisting she wasn't trying to improve her looks for Cooper.

"Don't we look pretty," she exclaimed, holding her daughter up to the dresser mirror as she brushed out the girl's nut-brown curls, loving the way they fell in perfect ringlets around her pixie face. Willow's own hair was straight as a stick and was so unremarkable she usually pulled it back in a ponytail.

As Lilybelle watched without expression, Willow blew raspberries against her three-year-old's neck, hoping for a spontaneous giggle or any sort of reaction. All the girl did was push her mother's face away. She grabbed the tattered plush rabbit she'd had since infancy and ran from the room. Willow heard the screen door slam. Would she ever break through Lily's barriers?

Willow shut her eyes for a moment, then dragged both her hands down her cheeks. They never used to look this sunken. Foregoing lipstick or blush which she hadn't used in so long she'd forgotten where she'd stashed the containers, Willow gave another twist to the rubber band holding her ponytail. Beauty products wouldn't help her run the ranch, so why bother? Exiting the room, she tracked after her daughter, although Willow knew exactly where she'd find her. On the porch, in her favorite corner.

She had no more than stepped out the door herself, still barefoot, when she saw Cooper trotting his big gelding right up to the steps. He vaulted out of the saddle and landed mere inches away from her. Flushing, Willow leaped backward and bumped into the wall.

"Sorry," Coop said, sounding breathless. "I got so caught up in surveying your land, I was afraid it'd be dark before I had a chance to try and repair the hose and fill the water tanks—wow, you smell good," he said. "Like sugar cookies."

"Vanilla," she corrected, sidling farther away. "It's my shampoo."

Coop wrinkled his nose. "I don't blame you for shying away from me. I've been out in the sun for hours. I should have stopped for a dip in your pond."

"You probably still can. It stays light longer now that summer's here. What's the verdict on other projects after the hose?" she asked.

"I don't have to tell you the whole place is in poor shape." Removing his hat, Coop raked a hand through his sweat-damp hair, standing the almost-black locks on end. "A good, all-around cowhand could improve this place immensely, you want someone who can paint, do fence repair, fatten cattle and maybe break the wild colt I spotted in your high pasture—which by the way needs new seed in the worst way. It'd take about three to four weeks, but it's all stuff that'll attract prospective buyers much faster."

"Three to four weeks?" Willow gasped and clutched a hand to her throat. "Out of the question. I simply can't afford that. I need to sell fast, though. Or failing that, get the steers to market. I'm tempted to do that and let the ranch go back to the bank."

"Then what will you do, Willow? Go live with your mom? I know your dad passed away the year I left town. I was scheduled for a rodeo at the time," he mumbled, adding belated condolences.

"At least Dad's no longer suffering. And, no, I can't move in with Mom. She's remarried. To a man she met through friends. They live in East Texas, in the Piney Woods. Working two jobs for as long as she did, while taking care of Dad, she deserves to kick back and be happy without me underfoot."

"Seems to me that you did more caregiving than she did. But, hey, this ranch won't be half the work once it's spruced up. If you don't have anyplace to go…" He tugged an ear, letting his sentence trail.

"I'd have to raise *something* to make the ranch pay, Cooper," she said. "But I can't. I don't have money for seed. And the bottom line is I need a job that'll allow me to spend more time with Lilybelle. We need to move to a city with access to services for special-needs children," she said, her eyes straying to the child rocking herself where she crouched in one corner of the porch. "My daughter is autistic," Willow revealed quietly. Cooper could see her lips tremble visibly even though she looked away.

Chapter Three

Coop's mind jolted, then went into free fall as he tried to process what Willow had just said. Would telling her he was sorry sound too trivial? Man, he hurt for her. Hurt also for the shy child who looked perfect, though petite for her age. Some part of that initial jolt came from hearing the child's name. *Lilybelle*. It was a name Willow had talked about when she and Cooper were serious. What she'd wanted to name their daughter if they ever had one. *Lily* for Coop's mother, and *Belle* for Willow's.

Coop was quite sure Willow named her daughter without informing Tate of the name's origins. Tate had no doubt left it up to her, as his own parents had separated in a bitter divorce before Willow moved to Hondo. But Coop let all of those issues pass without comment. Instead, he focused on the child's condition.

"Lord, Willow, it must be extra-difficult for you, knowing how hard it was to care for your dad all those years," he managed, his sympathetic gaze resting on the child. "I noticed she was shy with strangers, but I figured it was because you were protective of her, since you live way out of town and have no close neighbors."

"About the work that needs doing around here,"

Willow said, crossing her arms and getting back to business. "I can afford to pay you for two days' labor. The fence is probably the most important. I thought maybe you could set some of the posts deeper?"

Coop shifted his attention back to Willow. "With our history, I can't in good conscience charge you a dime."

She stiffened. It was plain at the outset that she intended to refuse. Coop wasn't surprised when she said, "I pay my way. I don't need your charity."

"Okay." He held up his hands. "I won't argue with you. I've got the time. You need a few things done. Pay me for fixing the fence. Then we'll see about doing the rest for room and board."

A wide range of emotions flitted across Willow's face before her too-thin shoulders sagged. "I'll agree to those terms provided you're okay with mine. You'll bunk in the barn, and I'll set breakfast and a sack lunch out on the porch. And the same with supper. If you want the night meal hot, be here to pick it up by seven. I have a hard-and-fast rule that no ranch hands are allowed inside my home. Ever."

"So I heard," Coop drawled, mentally kicking himself for not going with his first impulse of hightailing it out of there the moment he discovered who the widow was. It irked him that there was no trust between them, despite the fact that they'd once shared every intimacy. He wondered when she'd grown so hard and closed off. Granted, her life had never been a cakewalk, what with having an invalid father, and a mother who was never at home because she worked two jobs. But, hell, they'd been lovers, and now she was leery of letting him step inside her ramshackle house. Telling himself the sooner he blew through the chores and left her place, the better, Coop slapped his hat against his leg, bounded down the steps and scooped up the reins.

"Tonight's supper will be macaroni and cheese," Willow called. "We have that a lot because it's Lily-belle's favorite. I'll set out a covered plate in about an hour."

He gave a curt nod, then led his horse, Legend, away. He found it hard to be curt. Willow talked big, but she looked defenseless, standing there hunched, one bare foot tucked beneath the other. Willow and her delicate child, who'd stared at Coop out of big, wounded eyes.

In the barn, he asked himself again what he was getting into as he jerkily unsaddled his horse, but he shook off the thought, and set to work shoveling out two stalls for his animals. The barn was a mess he'd wait until morning to fully deal with.

He decided to sleep out under the stars that night, where it smelled better. And speaking of smelling better... He dragged the partially repaired hose behind the barn and did his best to fix up a makeshift shower, glad there wasn't anyone around to see him hop around or hear him curse the icy water. At least the shocking cold neutralized his lingering anger over Willow's standoffishness.

The shower made him late to pick up his dinner. It was nearly eight o'clock, but he was hungry enough to scarf down the congealed cheesy macaroni, and be thankful for it. The vegetable—zucchini—was less appetizing, but it helped fill the hole in his stomach. After he finished, he rinsed his plate and left it where he'd found it.

In the morning, he saw Willow and Lilybelle crossing the field that flanked the house. They disappeared over a rise, making no effort to contact him. *No big surprise there.*

Coop scavenged through the toolshed that sat adjacent to the barn, searching for what he'd need to mend the fences and shovel out the barn. He was astounded that the shed and tack room were both devoid of any of the tools one would expect to find on a ranch.

NOT CATCHING WILLOW at the house or elsewhere on the property for two days, Coop made do with the hammers, pliers and crowbar he carried in his pickup.

Like clockwork, his meals appeared on the porch outside the door. They proved to be as meager as the grain boxes Willow should have filled to begin fattening her steers for market. Coop didn't want to track her down and complain about the lack of anything resembling meat in any of his meals when it was clear that times were tough. Breakfast was usually pancakes, lunch was peanut butter and jelly sandwiches, and supper, a noodle dish with tomato sauce or white gravy.

Cooper was fed up by day three. By then it was readily apparent that Willow intended to pull out all the stops to avoid him, or send him away completely. At breakfast she'd set out an envelope with two days' pay in it and a note thanking him for his help. With that, he fired up his pickup and headed into town to hunt up a good restaurant and a feed store. He left the envelope full of cash where it was.

Not caring that it was barely ten o'clock in the morning, Coop went into a busy local café and ordered a steak with all the trimmings. Satisfied, he paid and gave the waitress a good tip. "Can you direct me to the closest feed store?" Coop asked her.

"Hank Jordan's is the only feed store serving our area," she said, drawing him a rough map on a napkin.

Coop arrived at the feed store to find Hank himself behind the counter.

"I'm doing some work for Willow Walker," Coop said. "I need twenty sacks of grain, two hundred-foot hoses and rye seed for a couple of fifty-acre fields. I assume Mrs. Walker runs a tab for essentials?"

"You assume wrong," Hank said, peering at Coop over a pair of wire-rimmed half-glasses. "You the latest of her part-timers? Last two guys came in and bought mash for their horses. Don't see much of the widow. Now, her husband was a piece of work. Had an excessive taste for gambling and booze, but he never seemed short of money. The missus rarely came to town, but when she did, she paid cash."

Coop frowned. "I'm actually an old friend of Mrs. Walkers. I haven't seen her since before she married Tate, but her ranch is a little the worse for wear, and I want to help her out."

"If you ask me, she shoulda left that no-good husband of hers a long time ago, but she stuck it out. You know how people in small towns talk. Well, I've heard from more than one source that while she was preg-

nant, she was seen with bruises. My wife, who sometimes cashiers here, said she noticed, and asked, but
was told they came from working cattle. No one bought
that story. And no one held any liking for her man, who
bragged that his dad, supposedly a wealthy rancher up
north, bought him this ranch and stocked it with prime
steers. If you and the widow go back a ways, you probably know more about the family than I do. One thing
I thought was odd—after the big brawl where Walker
was accidentally shot, his father swooped into town,
claimed his son's body, and took him elsewhere to be
buried. I figured he hasn't been providing for Mrs.
Walker 'cause she's been selling furniture and tools
for grocery money and to replenish her kettle ever since
the funeral. I hope you're what you say—a friend—and
it don't make things worse for her that I'm telling tales
out of school."

"No, no," Coop stammered. "I appreciate the information. I'll pay for the stuff I ordered. While you're
at it, if there's room in my pickup out there to add six
bales of hay, pile it on."

After his pickup was loaded, Coop backtracked to
the area's big-box store, which sold a little of everything. He was frustrated to think that, given their history, Willow hadn't come clean with him about her true
circumstances.

Forty minutes later, he came out with enough bags
of groceries to fill the passenger side of his Ram. He
fumed all the way back to Willow's ranch, telling
himself it was no wonder she looked as skinny as the
branches on the tree for which she was named.

On pulling into the driveway, he saw that her front door was open, except for the screen. Coop jumped out and quickly unloaded the many bags of groceries, transferring them to the porch. When he finished, he knocked loudly on the screen door casing, making a racket that brought Willow running.

"Cooper, what on earth?" She wiped her hands on a dish towel and unlatched the screen. "I thought you'd taken off without the pay I set out for you, but then I realized you'd left your horses and trailer behind. What's all this?" She swept a hand over the sacks of groceries, bending to pull Lilybelle back when she wriggled through the narrow opening.

Coop stood there holding two more large sacks. Pushing open the screen with one foot, he thrust them into Willow's arms. "I went to the feed store and tried to put a few items on your tab. Imagine my surprise," he said tightly, "when the owner said you don't run a tab, and only buy supplies when you have the cash. Seeing as how you've been feeding me the equivalent of rice and beans all week, I suggest it's time you were candid with me about what's really going on here." He didn't mean to sound gruff but couldn't help it. He grabbed up two of the heavier boxes and steamrolled into the house, stomping on into the kitchen ahead of her.

Coop let her stew silently while he brought in the remaining groceries. "Well," he said, opening the almost-empty fridge to shove in three gallons of milk and a variety of other perishables. "Start spilling your guts."

Willow braced her hands on the grocery-covered countertop. Appearing anxious, she sputtered and ended by saying defensively, "I never lied to you, Cooper. Everything I said was the truth. I told you Tate died last year, but I assumed you already knew. I admitted the ranch is too much work. And I do have it listed for sale. But what's to be gained by airing Tate's and my dirty laundry to you, of all people?"

"Why me *of all people?*" Coop asked, barely pausing as he opened cupboard doors and filled the shelves with cereal, bread, rice and various staples.

"Because of...oh, just because," she said, throwing up her hands. "Like you've never made a mistake in your life."

He laughed. "According to my brother I've made plenty. I sold my quarter horses, and I pissed away almost all of what I earned on the rodeo circuit."

"But you didn't—*you don't*—have a family to support. It's different for you, Coop," she said, her lips in a tight line.

"Tell me how." He merely stared at her, waiting.

Willow sank down on a kitchen chair and laced her hands together in front of her. Faking interest in her fingernails, she whispered, "With what you've been privy to these past few days, I'm reasonably sure you've guessed that while Tate liked being seen as a ranch owner, he disliked the work required to actually run a ranch."

"And...he lost valuable ranch profits playing poker?"

Willow opened her clasped hands to let Lilybelle climb onto her lap. Heaving a sigh, she mumbled into her daughter's hair, "Yes. Tate fancied himself a gambler. The truth is, he lost far more than he ever won. Money was always tight."

"Did you do all the work around here so he could gamble?"

She shook her head. "The bulk of what I've done was after his death. Before, his dad bought into Tate's lies about hardships. Rustlers. Sick cattle. Endless droughts. Bart got into the habit of sending a check the first of every month."

"He didn't come to evaluate things for himself?"

"No. Bart doesn't deal well with women. He didn't want Tate to marry me. They spoke on the phone... when his son was sober. Tate's other weakness was booze. The last two years, he drank a lot. I made sure I beat him to the mailbox so I could bank Bart's checks and pay Lily's doctor bills, pay for her tests and buy food before Tate emptied our account. I don't think he knew how much his dad sent, or that I forged his name on the checks to deposit them." She lowered her eyes to avoid Coop's laser stare, and reluctantly gave up the last bit of information. "It's been harder since Tate's death. Bart quit sending money."

"What did he expect you to do? How did he expect you to clothe and feed his grandchild?"

"Bart ignores the fact that Lily and I exist. His wife ran off, so he thinks the worst of all women. And Tate lied to him a lot."

"Bart's a jerk. He can afford to help you."

"Yes, well, I applied for Aid for Families with Dependent Children, and for food stamps," she said. "But because I had the ranch and still owned cattle, we didn't qualify—not even for farm subsidy because I wasn't growing crops to sell. But we got by," she said, squaring her shoulders.

"Right," Coop said huffily. "Selling the tools necessary for a working ranch. And furniture out of your house, I hear," he said, taking a brisk survey of the kitchen before stepping over to the doorway to check the living room. "And as if that wasn't bad enough, I heard he hit you."

"Great! So the town busybodies shared every crappy detail of my life. Well, I didn't ask you to ride in here on a white charger and save us, Cooper Drummond. We aren't your problem," she said coolly. "I put out two days' wages for you. So now you can take off. If you give me an address when you land at your next job, I'll send you repayment money for the groceries. I don't want you concerning yourself with us any longer."

"Bull! That was a nice little speech, Willow. Do you by any chance remember what you said to me right before I went to rodeo?"

She rolled her eyes. "Can it be repeated in front of a child?" She moved to place her hands over her daughter's ears. "I probably said a lot of mean things, Cooper. I didn't want you to go. I felt…cut adrift, and I couldn't understand why you'd choose to go off and ride in rodeos."

"You never asked me to stay. What you said as I left, was that I was the most stubborn, pigheaded guy you'd ever had the misfortune to meet."

"I didn't want to…hold you back," she persisted. Then, noticing he'd pulled a large box of graham crackers out of a sack, she met his eyes. "Graham crackers? How did you know they're Lily's favorite snack? We'd run out of them," she added, biting her lip.

"I had no idea, Willow. I figured all kids like them."

For the first time since barging into her house, Coop felt self-conscious. "Hey, I bought Miss Lilybelle something else. I almost forgot." He snapped his fingers. "If you think it's okay for her to have these." He pulled out a cloth bag tied closed with a drawstring. "Blocks," he said. "They're big, bright colorful ones. You can use them to teach her numbers and letters." He tumbled several blocks onto the table.

"Oh, Coop." Willow choked up, unable to manage anything else for a moment. She drew her chair closer to the table and started to hand a block to Lilybelle, then saw that the child had beaten her to it, grabbing one in each hand. In the blink of an eye, Lily sorted and stacked all the blocks lying on the table by color.

"Look at that, will you?" Coop grinned as he dumped out the rest of them.

"I'm amazed." Willow gaped at the girl. "I hadn't tried blocks. I... Coop, thank you. I've been really rude to you and you're nothing but nice to me."

"I want to stay here and finish some of the other things on your to-do list. Don't make a big deal out of it, Willow. I saw the blocks while I was out and thought of the kid. I bought the groceries because I'd like to eat something besides the same old pasta disguised in a variety of thin sauces."

Willow stood Lily on her feet, then rose to glare at Coop. "Those meals weren't that bad. And my sauces aren't thin."

"But *you* are. So I rest my case."

Willow tossed her head. "Back when you took off for the rodeo, did I also tell you that you're the bossiest person I'd ever met?"

"Not that I recall. I think I'm very reasonable."

"Bossy! I'm not going to be your short-order cook, Coop. But since you were so kind as to fill my fridge and cupboards, pray tell me what your heart desires for your evening meal," she said saucily.

He rolled his eyes. "I didn't buy this stuff to make your life more difficult, Willow. You choose something out of what I bought. But please, put a little meat in whatever you fix." He headed for the door, then stopped. "Uh, you haven't become a vegetarian, have you? The way I remember it, you used to make a tasty pot roast. Oh, and burgers. Nice, fat ones." He gathered up the empty grocery sacks and carried them to the screen door. Calling back over his shoulder, he said, "And meat loaf. You made a damn fine meat loaf, Willow."

Willow wasn't quick enough with a retort, though he probably wouldn't have heard, anyway, as the screen door banged shut in his wake. She leaned a shoulder against the edge of the kitchen doorway. For several minutes she did nothing. It wasn't until she shook herself alert that she realized she'd been smiling. Something she hadn't done much of over the past several years. It felt unfamiliar. But good, too, she thought as she turned and saw that Lily had stacked the blocks in neat rows, not only by color, but with the letters all facing the refrigerator. Willow's heart nearly burst with hope and pride and gratitude to Coop. Lord, he was a good man.

So, why did she want him to leave? Why did she feel such guilt over his landing on her doorstep? She had plenty of answers, but she needed to keep them to herself. Anything else would be unfair to the man she'd pushed out of her life five years ago.

Chapter Four

The back of Cooper's pickup still needed to be unloaded. Feeling he'd made some headway in dealing with Willow, Coop whistled a decent rendition of Jimmy Buffett's "Margaritaville." It was a catchy tune he liked to pick out on his guitar—which was stashed behind the Ram's backseat. Maybe he'd take it up to the porch tonight and play a little after supper. Willow and Lilybelle might like that.

While he was at the big-box store, he'd cruised through the book and magazine department, and spotted a health magazine containing a couple of articles on autism. He'd skimmed one to see if it'd give him any insight into Willow's daughter. One article, written by a parent of an autistic boy, mentioned that he responded positively to piano tunes. The kid was quite a bit older than Lily; he owned a CD player and an iPod, on which his parents downloaded music for him. Coop bought the magazine, since he wanted to do more than just skim both articles. The other one was written by a neurologist, and it looked informative. He was trying to understand more about the illness. Or was it called a condition? A disorder? He wasn't even sure what to call it. Not that Willow would welcome him sticking his nose into her family business. She used to be so open and talkative. Now she kept anything personal to herself. He'd had to drag the story on Tate out of her, even though it was common knowledge in town.

Thinking about Tate ruined Coop's mood. Physical labor was the best for flushing any thoughts of that jerk right out of his mind.

He unloaded the hay bales, breaking a couple open and spreading them around the stalls in the barn where he'd stabled his horses. He filled a third one, where he'd bed down now that the old barn smelled better. Fresher.

Too bad he didn't have access to a tractor so he could haul the feed sacks out to the feed troughs. Hoisting one up onto his shoulder and jogging it over to where the majority of the steers milled about, it occurred to him that when he'd finished this chore he might be too tired to eat. The work took him until late afternoon. The thought of having to repeat this every day until Willow's cattle fattened up was almost enough to make him rethink staying around. No wonder Willow looked like a toothpick if she was the one who hauled hay to her herd. He had to hand it to her. She had grit.

Back at the pickup, he dusted off and eyed the sacks of seed he'd bought to resow the two main fields for fall. Was it even worth doing? A closer inspection of what passed for an irrigation system was discouraging. All the sprinkler heads were rusted or corroded, and a few were missing. And the job of spreading the seed, which—given the size of her fields—ought to take a matter of hours, would probably take days, thanks to the absence of a tractor and spreader. He'd seen a handbroadcaster in the barn. Standing with his forearms draped on the side of the pickup bed, he recalled all the up-to-date equipment owned by the Triple D. Coop calculated the unlikelihood of Sully's lending him a tractor, plow, spreader and harrow for a few days. Plus he'd need one of the Triple D's flatbed trucks and trailers to bring it down here from Hondo. About a hundred miles each way. He slapped his hat against his thigh and snorted in disgust. It was a pipe dream. He'd have to apologize for socking Sullivan, if not actually grovel for leaving their ranch in the lurch for five years. Groveling didn't come easy to him. And that punch to Sully's jaw had been a long time coming.

Coop squinted into the waning sun. He wasn't ready to swallow his pride and kiss Sully's boots yet. It'd take more than a few days of backbreaking work to get him in that frame of mind.

He stacked the bags of seed outside the barn, rinsed out the bed of his truck, then took the hose around back, where he washed off the day's grime and sweat. He had only two more clean sets of clothes in his duffel. He should have taken his laundry to town when he went. He'd seen Willow hanging their clothes on a line out back, so she must not own a dryer. He'd hunt up a Laundromat in the next day or so.

The smell of the evening meal wafting down to the barn reached Coop half an hour prior to the time Willow had told him his meals would be waiting for him. He knew before he tucked in his shirt, pulled on his boots and retrieved his guitar for the trek to the house that she was fixing her signature meat loaf....

Coop had shared enough of the meals Willow had fixed for her father to identify the aroma. He'd hung out after school sometimes, talking rodeo with her dad. She almost never came to his house. They were three men living alone and her mom didn't think it was proper.

Coop's mouth was watering long before he bounded up the steps of Willow's porch.

She was just setting out the covered plate on an orange crate next to the door.

"Oh, Cooper, here you are. I saw you packing a lot of feed out to the cattle. I was worried you'd be late and would have to eat reheated supper. Hey, let me bring out a chair so you can take a load off while you eat. You must be exhausted from everything you did today. Those feed sacks weigh a ton. It's why I haven't tried to fatten up the steers."

Coop propped his guitar case against the porch railing. "The thought of a good meal brought me running, Willow. I've been tortured by the smell of your meat loaf from about the time it went into your oven. *Tantalized* is a better word," he added quickly, catching the look of dismay that crossed her face.

"Here I figured I'd surprise you...."

Coop picked up the plate and removed the cover. "It looks as delicious as I remember. And fresh peas in their pods. And cornbread. You exceeded my wildest expectations, Willow."

She chuckled, and he noticed a dimple he remembered well, one he hadn't seen since his arrival. All too fast, though, she blushed and retreated into the house.

"Wait," he called, unable to stop himself. "Why don't you bring out plates for you and Lily, too? We'll call it a picnic."

Willow didn't respond immediately and Coop

couldn't see through the screen into the darkened house. But then she cracked it open and said, "Lily's already eaten. She only likes a few foods right now." Willow glanced away. "That's part of her disorder. Some forms of autism have an obsessive component. For instance, she'll like one food, one shirt, one pair of pajamas, and it's a battle to get her to change. Today she dug in the dirt the whole time I weeded what's left of my garden. That tired her out, so she ate, had her bath and crashed early. But I, um, suppose I can eat out here." She glanced back when Coop said nothing. "Why the frown? Was the invitation only for the two of us?"

"What? Oh, no. It's just that I brought my guitar with me tonight. I read something in a magazine about a boy with autism responding well to music. Not that I'm a great guitarist," he pointed out. "And I know next to nothing about autism."

"I wish I knew more. Every expert, every doctor and every therapist has a different theory," she said. "But you used to be good enough on the guitar to play in that band during college. And, Coop, it's thoughtful of you to think of Lily. She loves the blocks you bought. But I'd really like to hear you play for a while tonight."

"Great, but please hurry and dish up your food. I can't wait to dive into this while it's hot."

"Dig in. Don't wait for me." Willow was quick, however. And even at that, Coop had sampled everything on his plate before she returned to take a seat two steps below him. "I intended to get you a chair, but you seem to be doing all right without it. Be careful leaning against that post, though. I noticed some of them are rotting at the base. From the weather, I guess."

Turning, he inspected the one at his back. "Looks like two or three posts and part of the foundation will need to be replaced before we can paint the place. I didn't pick up any paint this trip, but I can get new boards and paint next time. You'll need to go to town with me to choose a color."

"Cooper." Willow paused and shook her head, a forkful of food halfway to her mouth. "What part of *I don't have the money to make all these repairs or to cover the stuff you've already bought* don't you understand? I thought we already had this discussion."

"This is the best meal I've had in weeks," he said, ignoring her. "Is there any more cornbread? No, don't get up. I'll help myself. Is it in the oven or on the back of the stove?"

"I left the pan in the oven, which is still warm. Coop, we are going to talk about the amount you spent today and set a schedule for me to repay you. You cannot change the subject whenever it suits you or because you want to avoid talking about something. I remember you always used to do that to get your way. It's still annoying."

He came back with a chunk of cornbread for each of them. "I think gray with a dark blue trim would look good back here next to those oaks, don't you?" he asked in a thoughtful voice.

"Cooper Drummond!" Willow's exasperation was unmistakable.

He grinned as he waved a fork in the air. "This house isn't all that big. I can rent a power sprayer and clean the siding, get rid of the moss and mildew in an hour or two. It'll dry while I return the rig, and if we both paint, we can get it done in no time. I knew a couple of guys on the circuit who sold their homes, and they told me that for every dollar they invested in painting and so on, they made back three when they sold. You've never said what you plan to do once you sell, but you did say something that suggested you might move somewhere you can get more help for Lily. Everything costs more in the city so you'll need to get as much as you can for the ranch."

She dug a crater in what remained of her meat loaf. "I don't recall mentioning anything like that. What did I say? And when?"

"It was vague." Coop gestured with his cornbread, then chewed and swallowed a bite before answering. "And I'm reasonably sure better programs are available in someplace like San Antonio. Carrizo Springs is a nice town, but I doubt it's a high-tech center for the latest and greatest in innovative medicine."

"Your point is?" She set her plate aside and leaned back against the opposite post, closing her eyes.

Coop probed further. "Is there a treatment for autism? If so, what all is involved?"

"I don't know," she said. "It's a disorder with many facets. I first noticed something was wrong when Lilybelle was around two." Willow rubbed a thumb over her palm. "I told our doctor about my concerns when Lily began to withdraw. She started that rocking with her stuffed rabbit, which was suddenly the only toy she had any interest in. Not that she owned a lot of toys, but she had a doll, and books she'd loved." Willow stopped, a catch in her voice.

Coop waited, then finally prompted, "So, this local doctor sent you to a therapist?"

"No. He sent us to a specialist in San Antonio. They did tests. ABA, they call them—applied behavior analysis. Tate was upset about the cost. All they could really tell me was that she's developmentally delayed and has impaired communication, which I already knew. It wasn't until a visiting nurse came to the house that the word *autism* was attached to Lilybelle. My heart nearly stopped. The nurse could tell, and since the specialist hadn't labeled Lily, she arranged for a cognitive therapist, who spent an hour assessing Lily before writing a list of things I was supposed to do. Repetitive play. Exercise. Reading from the same book every night. Keeping to an exact schedule. Setting a structured environment. She said fewer girls have autism than boys do. But one in every hundred and ten children are born with some form of it."

"That's a lot," Coop commented.

Willow nodded. "I tried to follow her suggestions. But I spent most of my day doing chores, and I took Lily with me when I fed and watered the cattle. At the end of the day, we were both too tired to look at any of her books. And she gets cranky when she wants to sleep."

"Did the therapist only come that one time?"

"Twice. The second visit, she brought information about a school in Austin that has a program for kids from age two to adulthood. The tuition costs a mint. There are scholarships, but the kids live there. It's not the only school, of course. All big cities have them, I guess. Tate was in favor of sending her if he didn't have to pay." She paused. "He rarely interacted with her. He told the therapist Lily wasn't his daughter. He even said that to his dad. Tate and I got into a huge fight over that. Anyway, the therapist left, said she'd be back in a week and that she'd bring the papers to apply for funding. I went and packed for Lily and me. We had a second car then. I drove off, but Tate came after us in the pickup. He ran me off the road and dragged us back. Then he sold my car. Things were tense between us before, but they spiraled downhill after that. I fired the therapist to keep her from bringing the papers. Tate stayed too drunk to realize what I'd done. It was like we were his possessions. He had a dog-in-the-manger attitude when it came to me." Willow's eyes filled with tears.

Coop felt a painful wrench to his heart, yet some part of his brain nagged that she should've known better than to marry Tate Walker. That started a war inside his head. Like a damned fool, he'd taken off to do his thing with the rodeo, and as Willow had accused the other day, he'd abandoned her. A touch of his old pride surfaced, dictating that he not ask her why she hadn't cared enough to wait until he got riding broncs out of his system. But was that fair of him? Damn, he wished he could let go of the past.

"Are you finished eating?" she asked, breaking into his moody thoughts.

"Uh, yeah, sure. Can I help carry this stuff in? Lend a hand with dishes?"

"Heavens, no." Leaping up, Willow collected her

plate and his. "You've done enough today. Anyway, didn't you say something about playing some tunes? I can hear you from the kitchen. It'll make my job go faster, and I'll bring out a pitcher of sweet tea when I'm done. Unless you'd prefer coffee? I saw you bought a big can. I still can't drink the stuff."

"I developed a taste for it on the road. You wouldn't believe the number of miles I drove getting from rodeo A to B to C. It's a hard habit to break."

"Driving from rodeo to rodeo? Or guzzling coffee?" she asked, pausing at the screen.

He rose and opened it for her. "The coffee," he answered.

Willow entered the house, and peered back over one shoulder, a smile teasing the corners of her lips. "Thanks for getting the door. I'm not used to having a gentleman around."

"Don't ever compare me to Tate, Willow." The words came out like a growl.

"I...I...I'd never do that, Coop. You two are as different as night and day. But if you tracked me down expecting an apology for old mistakes, hell will freeze over first."

"I didn't track you down, Willow. Didn't you see how shocked I was that first day? All this time, have you been thinking I looked you up for—why would I?"

She shook her head. "For revenge? Men are such sore losers. So, yes, it's crossed my mind that your shock was an act. You see, I stopped believing in serendipity, Santa Claus and the tooth fairy a long time ago."

"Huh?" Coop scratched his head.

"Never mind," she snapped, hating that she'd almost told him how often she'd gazed up at the stars at night, foolishly wishing he'd show up out of the blue and sweep her away from her sorry life. She *wanted* him to have tracked her down, darn it. "If you're going to play your guitar, then play," she said. "Otherwise, I'll lock up, put the dishes to soak overnight and go to bed."

He gave up trying to sort between the lines of what she'd said. "I'll play for a while, as long as you don't expect Keith Urban. I've only played a few times since I left Jud Rayburn's ranch. It takes regular practice, so I'm not sure how good I'll be."

"What were you doing at Rayburn's? Doesn't his land abut the Triple D?"

"It does. I wanted to get back in the swing of everything that needs doing on a large working cattle ranch. In a way I thought it might help me decide whether to present myself to Sully at the Triple D. Like I told you, we fell out. After our last big row, I quit on Jud and rode south. I couldn't find steady work, but I kept hearing about a woman, a widow out of Carrizo Springs, with a spot for an all-around cowhand. Funny, nobody told me your name."

"Ah. Would you have come by here if someone had?"

Coop rubbed a thumb back and forth over his jaw, then paused, realizing he badly needed a shave. "To tell you the truth," he said slowly, after several moments had passed. "I don't know that I would have, Willow."

She bit her lip. "I appreciate your honesty, Coop." Then she disappeared, jerking the screen door out of his loose grasp.

Coop wished he'd lied and told her he would've come, anyway. But he really wasn't sure. Especially after taking into account the roller-coaster ride his feelings had been on since he'd first seen her. And the question he probably ought to be asking himself wasn't whether or not he would've come, but why he felt so damned compelled to stay.

Sinking back down on the porch steps, Coop unsnapped his case, took out the guitar and rippled a thumb over the strings, stopping to tune the ones that had jiggled loose on the drive. A big pickup with enough power to pull a two-horse trailer wasn't the smoothest ride for a sensitive guitar.

Jimmy Buffett's songs were still on his mind, so he started with "Margaritaville," then moved into "Son of a Son of a Sailorman." Coop liked honky-tonk best; some tunes just freed a guitar picker's mind. That was the case tonight, and he'd almost forgotten where he was when the screen door opened and Willow backed out carrying a tray with a pitcher of icy tea and a pair of frosty glasses.

Coop hit a loud, flat chord. Willow had changed into a pair of worn-looking jean shorts and a loose, flowing blouse. Once again he noticed that her slender feet were bare. For a minute that seemed to stretch on forever, he stared at her.

She bent and carefully set the tray on the orange crate, then filled both glasses—giving Coop a leisurely time to study her long, nicely suntanned legs and narrow ankles. Old desires churned inside him.

"Why did you stop playing?" she asked, turning to face him as she passed him a glass.

"I, ah, can't drink and play at the same time," he said, tripping over the words; to his chagrin, he nearly let the cold glass slip through his clammy fingers.

Willow picked up her own glass and reclaimed her seat two steps down. "Drink up," she said. "I really enjoyed the serenade. I hope you don't mind that I took the time to change into something cooler."

Coop couldn't speak so he just shook his head while he gulped his drink.

"My kitchen is so tiny. Using the oven in the summer makes the whole room feel like a sauna. Same with washing dishes in hot water. Even if Tate had been inclined to buy me a dishwasher—or a microwave, for that matter—there's no room to put one."

Coop found that listening to Willow talk about Tate while he'd grown hard with desire for her had the immediate effect of being doused in ice water. He drained his glass and, with some difficulty, climbed to his feet. He plopped the empty glass on the tray with force enough to draw Willow's attention.

She clambered up with less grace as she tried to avoid Coop, who banged around returning his guitar to its case, and struggled to keep her almost full glass upright.

"Coop?" She sounded hesitant, and in the dim light cast by the lone porchlight, he could see confusion mixed with inquisitiveness.

His voice was tight as he said, "Supper was great, and I'm glad we discussed Lilybelle's condition, but I draw the line at ruining an otherwise nice evening by listening to you complain about Tate. If you need a pal for that kind of heart-to-heart, I'm not your man,

Willow." Taking the steps in two bounds, he stalked across the yard and disappeared into the gloom of night.

She stood without moving as the crickets renewed their chirping. The hand that held her glass shook. *What had she said about Tate?* She couldn't remember. Earlier, Coop had sounded as if he knew all about her and Tate. She so rarely got to talk to anyone that having this opportunity to kick back and relax with Coop had been a treat. Tears welled in her eyes and spilled over. Now she'd have to go back to weighing every word, like she'd done with her husband. And that was supposing Cooper wasn't angry enough to leave. But, darn it, what right did he have to lecture her? Hadn't she told him not to stick around?

Willow clung to that thought as she picked up the tray to take it inside. Realistically, no possible good could come of Cooper's staying here. But for a while tonight she'd felt more lighthearted than she had in years. Was it so wrong of her to revel in a few moments of normalcy?

Perhaps she didn't deserve to have Coop back in her life....

She went inside and, after depositing the tray in the kitchen, made her way to bed without turning on the light. She lay watching the play of moonlight flickering between her bedroom curtains far into the night, her mind a jumble of too many might-have-beens. Her head was clear about not wanting to get involved with Cooper Drummond. It was her heart that was unwilling to let go.

Chapter Five

The morning after he'd stormed off Willow's porch in a huff, Coop's thoughts were still scattered. He felt bad for lashing out at her, but he couldn't abide hearing her talk about Tate. He didn't even want to hear her complain about the man. Part of him couldn't understand why she hadn't found a way to leave the SOB. She said he'd run her off the road once and then dragged her back to the house. That was one time. However, if Tate spent as many hours in town drinking and gambling as Willow indicated, couldn't she have asked for someone's help in getting away?

Willow wasn't weak-willed. She was a smart, savvy woman. And she wasn't a novice at navigating her way through government bureaucracies. Her mother, Belle, wasn't the one who'd researched and found a senior-care center to look after Marvin so Willow could attend college. Willow herself had done that.

Rolling out of bed, Coop got dressed. He skipped breakfast, heading straight out to the far corner of the property instead. He decided to tackle replacing mangled metal fence stakes that held up the wire sections and kept the cattle contained. It was a job that fit his mood today. The ground was half caliche, and

Willow said she wanted the stakes to go deeper, so he drove them in with brute force, swinging a fifty-pound sledgehammer. Coop put his whole back into the job, and each strike of hammer on metal sent a ripple of pain along his straining muscles. But somehow it was satisfying to imagine that he was driving Tate Walker's spirit farther into perdition.

After a while Coop developed a rhythm and was able to blank his mind to the pain, and to idle thoughts of Tate or Willow. Noon came, then marched past like one of the four-foot wire sections snaking along the perimeter of her ranch.

All at once she appeared in Coop's line of vision. Seeing her so suddenly caught him off guard. It broke his stride, forcing him to recognize that he was very near to dropping in his tracks. Sweat from the sun high overhead pasted his last clean chambray shirt to his aching back.

"What's up? I'm busy here." Coop whipped off his hat, wiped his brow with one hand and realized a row of blisters had sprouted along the base of his fingers. He tried to will them away, but it even hurt to fan his face with his hat, so he let the summer Stetson fall into the dirt. A few steers stood in a huddle nearby, their ropy tails swishing at flies. Coop waited impatiently for her to speak.

"I brought lunch," Willow said. "You skipped breakfast. Whatever demons are behind your assault on this fence, Coop, I can't stand by and watch you kill yourself."

"You said fixing this fence is my number-one priority." Afraid that he might pass out, Coop dropped to his haunches and leaned his wrists heavily on the three-foot sledge handle, silently praying for earth, sky and Willow to stop revolving in front of his eyes.

"Here, drink some water. You're white around your lips. Are you *trying* for sunstroke?" Willow removed a thermos from the basket she'd set at her feet and filled the lid with water.

Taking the cup with a shaking hand, Coop bent his head and dumped the cool water over his sweat-matted hair. The move put him on a level with Lilybelle, who had accompanied Willow and now peered solemnly at Coop from behind her mother's thigh. He imagined an old soul staring at him out of the girl's unblinking green-flecked eyes. Eyes that chastised him, or at least that was how it appeared to him. *How could he gripe at Willow in front of her kid?*

Regret tightening his chest, Coop turned his face up to Willow. "I appreciate lunch. Give me a second to get on my feet again and make my way over to the shade of that tree. I hope you brought enough food for us to share."

She pried the cup from his fingers. Picking up the tea towel that covered the basket, she passed it to Coop, indicating he should towel his hair and face. But as he took it from her, she spotted his blisters. A hiss of air escaped her lips. "You're finished for the day, Galahad. If we don't treat those blisters now, you're asking for infection. Where are your gloves, anyway? I thought bronc riders bought them by the case."

Getting up, Coop gingerly opened and closed both fists. "I have gloves in the barn in my saddlebags, along with liniment and witch hazel. I wasn't riding broncs today, so I guess I didn't think I'd need 'em."

Willow snorted. "Seems to me a horse tossed you on your head one too many times, Drummond."

He looked sheepish, but was gallant enough to reach for the basket.

Willow smacked the top of his hand lightly. "I get that you're a gentleman, okay? But if you tear those blisters open on this wicker handle, you'll be one *miserable* gentleman." She hefted the basket and took Lily's hand.

"Thanks, but I'm not used to being fussed over. I'll slap gauze packs across my hands and use gloves tomorrow." Even as he said this, he raised his right arm jerkily and rotated it from the shoulder, grimacing as he did.

"That is, if you can crawl out of bed in the morning," Willow said, skepticism on her face.

When they got to the old live oak, Coop eased his aching body down to the ground and carefully leaned his back against its wide trunk.

Willow, who'd retrieved his hat when he'd left it lying in the dirt beside the fence, set it beside him. Then she took a small blanket from the basket, followed by Lily's worn bunny rabbit. The girl immediately sat on the blanket, grabbed her stuffed toy and began to rock.

"What will you do if that toy falls apart?" Coop asked casually.

"Bite your tongue," Willow said, then sighed. "I honestly don't know. It was a gift my mother sent when Lilybelle was born. The chances of finding another one exactly like it are slim to none." She pulled wrapped sandwiches, a couple of apples and a plastic container of cut vegetables out of the basket. She offered Lily half a peanut butter and jelly sandwich; when the girl shook her head in refusal, Willow set the sandwich on a napkin. Passing Coop a tuna-salad sandwich and the container of veggies, Willow dropped into a cross-legged position. "A nurse at the neurologist's office where Lily was tested gave me a booklet that explained some behaviors that are common to kids diagnosed on the autism spectrum. Some kids react positively or negatively to textures, tastes, smells, et cetera. Lily likes the feel of the rabbit's chenille body. She likes soft cotton, flannel sheets and even the satin blanket edging."

Coop nodded as he bit into the sandwich. Once he'd swallowed, he said, "That's not so abnormal. I like my jeans broken in. And I dislike new shirts. I'm happier after they've been washed a hundred times."

"I don't think you'd go naked rather than wear something brand-new," Willow said wryly. "Lilybelle would do exactly that. Following her trail of discarded clothing through the house used to be a morning ritual."

"Why her, Willow? Why your daughter? Is autism genetic? Have there been other instances in your family? Or in the Walkers'?" Coop questioned as he unwrapped a second sandwich Willow had passed him. "Wouldn't surprise me if it was them," he muttered.

"The experts can't agree on a cause, Coop. It'd give you a headache if you tried to sift through all the studies out there. Practically every specialist has a different opinion." Willow rested her elbows on her knees and rubbed her face.

Coop hated seeing her look so distressed. "Hey, you have to eat, too. There's no end to the work that needs doing around here. If I'm gonna knock off on the fence for the rest of today, it'd be the perfect time for us to go to town and rent that power washer and for you to choose paint colors."

"You don't listen, Coop," she scolded. "Think of the rumors you've already heard about me. If you and I went to pick out house paint together, the whole town will believe Tate's lies about me being a flirt... or worse."

"They know he was full of crap. But there's nothing that says we need to shop in Carrizo Springs. I thought we could go to Crystal City. It's not that far away."

"There's still the cost, Cooper."

He idly polished an apple on his shirt. It sounded crisp as he bit into it.

Willow sat there, unable to read his expression.

Coop chewed, then swallowed before he addressed her concerns. "If you can't or won't accept my help for yourself, Willow, do it for Lily. You said there's more that could be done for her away from here. Selling the ranch will give you options."

"Damn you, Cooper! That's sneaky. I'll admit Lily is my weakness."

He almost said *And you're mine,* but was able to check his response. He hid the feelings racing through him by taking another bite of the juicy apple. *Appropriate,* he thought with chagrin. She was like Eve in the Garden of Eden. But no way would he be her Adam!

Climbing stiffly to his feet, he threw the apple core as far as he could, but almost cried out from the pain that cost him.

"Are you okay?" Willow asked softly.

"Fine. These old bones are just a bit rusty and not used to hard labor," he joked.

She laughed briefly. "You haven't changed. You always were quick to play on a girl's sympathy."

"Says the woman who insisted my hands needed doctoring."

"Right. And we're going to take care of them before we drive to Crystal City," she ordered briskly.

"Does the little squirt have a booster seat?"

Guilt flashed in Willow's eyes. "We had to have an infant car seat to bring her home from the hospital. It's not good, I know, but since she outgrew it, and I only have the old pickup that used to be Tate's, I have to buckle her in beside me any time I go to town. I don't go often," she added.

"I gathered that. A booster seat is something else to put on our list, then," Coop said.

"Cooper, once we tally up everything I'm going to owe you, I'll have to work two jobs somewhere else to pay you. Unless I can get a decent price for the cattle."

"We'll deal with it after I fatten those steers and we check out the best prices. Now, I want to see you eat that last sandwich as we walk back to the house." Coop pressed the sandwich into her hand. Then, seeing that Lily was eating hers, he sat back down and waited until they were both finished. He watched Willow wet a napkin with water from the thermos to wipe jelly off her daughter's face and hands. His stomach knotted.

Willow, who'd spent so much of her life taking care of her invalid father had loved to socialize during their college years. Now she was back to being dead serious about life again. It didn't seem fair. But who said life was fair?

AS THEY APPROACHED the house, Willow told Coop to grab any gauze pads he had on hand. "I'm not sure what's in my medicine cabinet," she admitted.

He headed to the barn and she to the house to return the picnic basket. He took time to wash up and change clothes, then met her on the porch. "Oh, these are good, thick pads," she said, taking the box out of his first aid kit, and motioning for him to sit on the top step.

She knelt and bent over his hands to inspect them. Coop noticed that she'd brushed out her ponytail and had changed her blouse, as well. The tips of her fine blond hair tickled his cheek as she worked on his hand. The combination of a light perfume, the feel of her hair and her soothing fingers caused a tightening in Cooper's groin. Old emotions swept over him in a rush. He might have touched her cheek and blown everything if she hadn't poured witch hazel over his blisters. The sting in two of the open blisters brought him straight up off the step.

"Holy...cheesecake!" he shouted, revising the last part of his curse as he jerked his hand out of Willow's.

"Sorry." Rocking back on her heels, she studied him with darkening eyes. "I didn't realize you'd broken any of the blisters."

He waved his hand and gritted his teeth, because he saw Lily gazing at him as she gripped her mother's arm. "It's okay," he assured the child. "Took me by surprise, is all." He could've said it was a surefire way of cooling a man's jets. And that was just as well. It was a good thing he hadn't acted on his impulse to touch Willow. He'd gone without a woman about as long as he ever had; that explained his reaction to her nearness. Or so he told himself while Willow finished bandaging his wounds.

She stood and put the tape, remaining gauze pads, antiseptic and scissors back into the kit before setting it down on the orange crate. "I'll leave this here because we'll need to change the bandages again in the morning. And tomorrow, wear gloves, okay?"

Nodding, Coop flexed his fingers. "They'll be fine in a day or two. I've had worse—like the rope burns I got from riding a really rank bucker. One sawed clear through my leather glove," he said. "I've known bronc riders who lost fingers if they got thrown and had the rope wrapped too tight."

She shuddered. "See, that's why I never understood why anyone could be so enamored of rodeo."

"It's the thrill of pitting yourself against a thirteen-hundred-pound animal. Or in the case of bull-riding, maybe two thousand pounds."

"Where's the thrill in getting maimed for life—or worse, killed?"

Turning toward her as they walked to his pickup, Coop spread his arms with a cocky grin. "I give you exhibit A. Do I look maimed or dead?"

Willow's eyes drifted over him from head to toe. "The question is, can you stay away from rodeo? Mom told me Dad quit when I was born. That thrill you talk about lured him back. I doubt it was worth spending the next twenty years in a wheelchair."

Coop didn't say anything. He opened the Ram's door and let her settle Lily in the backseat. He boosted Willow into the front passenger seat, shocked by how light she felt. His hands almost spanned her slender waist. Coop was thankful he'd pulled on a pair of gloves, because her blouse rode up and otherwise his bare hands would have connected with her skin.

He was doing his best to hang on to his old anger and resentment, but things kept happening to boot out those feelings. He needed to draw a firm line. It was fine to help Willow out for old times' sake; it'd be pure folly to let himself get attached to her again. Coop wasn't sure he had it in him to ever totally forgive her for marrying Tate Walker mere weeks after Coop had kissed her goodbye.

He drove in silence, wrapped in his thoughts.

Content to have someone else in the driver's seat, Willow stared out the side window, where a blazing sun shimmered off the desert landscape. A trio of dust devils kicked up and danced across the road through the scrub brush bordering the highway.

The silence in the cab got to Coop first. He dropped the sunshade and pulled a CD from the holder clipped to his visor. Country music soon wailed from the Ram's oversize woofers. He adjusted the volume twice before he caught sight of Lily's head bobbing in time to Rascal Flatts's "I Melt." His shoulders finally relaxing a little, Cooper nudged Willow's arm. He motioned toward the backseat with his chin.

She turned. "I expected to see that she'd fallen asleep."

"No, she's feeling the music."

"I don't know, Coop. She rocks so much of the time. When I had a radio, I don't recall her ever stopping to listen to the music." Willow frowned. "It breaks my heart," she murmured, worrying her bottom lip between her teeth as she watched Lily.

The sorrow in her voice clutched at Coop's throat. When he was able to speak, he said, "I hate hearing you sound so defeated. You said there are places that treat kids with Lilybelle's disorder."

"I'm not sure *treat* is the right term. The school Ms. Baxter talked about has a curriculum focusing on special education for a variety of learning disabled kids. The children there weren't all autistic. Some were bipolar, dyslexic, had ADD, ADHD or Asperger's, which is actually high-functioning autism. I'm not convinced the rate of success they claim is accurate."

"Oh? Wouldn't success need to be measured and documented before they could advertise through medical communities?"

"Maybe." Willow rubbed at the small creases that had formed between her eyebrows. "It costs sixteen to eighteen thousand dollars a year for tuition."

Coop whistled through his teeth. "As much as a semester of college."

"So far out of my reach it's impossible to consider. Maybe that's why I seem defeated. I want what's best for her, but I'm short on hope lately."

"There's always hope," he said. Slowing down, Coop

navigated through Carrizo Springs, then sped up on the other side as he aimed for Crystal City.

Once more they let the music envelop them.

"Ah, good. They have a large department store," Coop said, pointing to a sprawling building on the outskirts of town. "We can get Lily's booster seat, check out paint supplies and maybe even get a power washer. Then I want to drop off my clothes at a Laundromat before we hunt up a paint store. I figure the clothes will be washed when we're done and I'll stuff them in a dryer while we find a place to have supper."

Willow's turned to stare at him. "You didn't say anything about eating here, Cooper. And you can wash your clothes at my house."

"What? You don't want a night off from slaving over a hot stove?"

"It's, uh, I've never tried to take Lilybelle to a restaurant, Coop. She doesn't always handle new situations well. They make her anxious. Sometimes I wish I could crawl inside her head and understand what's going on in there." She twisted one hand around the other, and Coop realized she had no rings on any of her fingers. Maybe she'd hocked her diamond along with all the other things she'd sold.

"I don't want to cause either of you any stress, Willow. I'm used to doing my laundry at a Laundromat. And don't worry—I didn't plan on candlelight and wine. We can get burgers and eat in the cab."

"Uh. Okay. I've...well, suffice it to say I'm not used to spur-of-the-moment trips into town. If I seem overwhelmed at times, it's because I am. It's not that I don't appreciate everything you're doing for me, Cooper."

Not certain that was true, Coop angled into a parking space and circled the pickup to open her door. He helped Willow down, then moved the seat forward and unbuckled Lily, planning to lift her out. The child reared back in fright, arched her back and bellowed.

"I didn't touch her," he said, glancing helplessly at Willow.

"I know." She shouldered him aside and reached into the pickup, murmuring reassuringly to the little girl until her sobs faded into hiccups. Only then was Willow able to lever the child out, into her arms.

Coop felt awkward, and it cut deep that he'd scared Lily through his unthinking carelessness.

Willow noticed how he nervously jiggled his keys, and how quickly he'd withdrawn. "You can't take it personally, Coop. It's simply another aspect of the resistance to change I mentioned earlier. Managing change of any kind takes hours, days, weeks, sometimes months of repetition. You startled her, that's all."

At the store's automatic entrance, Coop stood aside and let Willow pass. "Do you want a cart?" he asked. "We could get two and you can go choose a booster seat while I cruise through the equipment section for a power washer and the other things on our list."

"I'd rather not. This store is pretty big and I don't want to lose you," she said. In fact, Willow wanted Coop to decide how much he was willing to spend on a booster seat. In all her married life, purchases inevitably came down to price. It made her stomach churn to even think about Coop berating her in public like Tate always had. A little voice reminded her that Coop had said not to confuse him with Tate. How could she? Coop had never been anything but thoughtful and kind.

They went through the aisles fairly quickly despite the number of shoppers and all the displays crowding the store. Coop knew what he wanted equipment-wise. In the children's department, he found the booster seats, but immediately turned to Willow. "I'm not sure what we need here. It looks as if the booster seats all say seven years or seventy pounds."

Willow checked the manufacturers' tags Coop had indicated. "Some states have strict laws about car seats. Lily outgrew her infant seat a long time ago. Tate—uh, I'm sorry for bringing him up as I know you don't want me to mention him—but he said all the new laws were only about getting customers to spend more money."

Coop's lips thinned. "Seems to me the aim is to save lives. Do you want to have Lily sit in one so we can make sure the padded wings protect her head?"

Willow was able to get her to try three. Plainly the girl's preference was for the softest, most padded of the trio. She kept stroking the material. It was also top of the line and the most expensive. Willow remarked on that, then said, "Any one of them would work, Coop, and be better than the nothing we have now. You're not earning money at the moment. Anyway, it's not your responsibility to provide my daughter with a car seat."

"Dammit, stop saying stuff like that, Willow. I know what I can afford." Coop picked up the seat Lily liked. "This one offers the most protection, right? And shouldn't it last her the longest?"

Willow met Coop's searing gaze and all she saw there was a true desire for her opinion. "I think this one will work best because if she likes how it feels, she won't fuss about being strapped into it."

"Good!" Coop put it into the cart. "We're done here. Let's check out and find a Laundromat, a paint store, then food."

The checkout lines were long. Lily got antsy about standing between people and display cases. Coop noticed and pulled out the keys to his pickup. "No need for us all to be stuck here. I'll pay and meet you in the parking lot."

Grateful for his compassion, Willow flashed him a rare smile. As she herded her daughter out into the afternoon sun, it crossed her mind that this was how family life should have been. A husband and wife should discuss purchases reasonably, make decisions and pull together as a unit. She'd never had that. And still didn't, she lamented. She'd pushed him away five years ago, and he was only here temporarily now. It wouldn't be smart to rely on him too much.

Those thoughts returned forty minutes later as they stood in the paint store and debated the various paint swatches. "You said something about gray with blue trim," Willow told Coop. "I'm inclined to agree, but it boggles my mind to see how many shades of gray there are. I'm not usually this indecisive."

"Well, you're painting it to sell. It'd be more important to love the colors if this was a home you planned to live in forever."

"You're right. Then let's go with driftwood gray and Colonial blue." She gave the strips to a waiting clerk, and was again struck by a sense of warmth when he called them Mr. and Mrs. Drummond after a glance at

Coop's credit card. Willow held her breath, expecting him to set the guy straight. But Coop didn't, and the feeling of family persisted as they left with their paint, dropped his clothes in a machine at the Laundromat, then hunted up a fast-food hamburger place.

"I'll go order," Coop said after Willow made selections for her and Lily from the limited menu. "You pick a table you think will suit Lily B."

Willow chose one by the window and had settled in when a group of five young women piled out of a Suburban. Willow noted they all wore flashy western garb. Sparkling tees, studded jeans and expensive boots. Her attention was drawn to them as they burst through the door, totally carefree in their chatter and laughter.

Her interest was piqued when one woman with long black hair spotted Coop at the counter and squealed in delight, exclaiming, "You're Cooper Drummond, this year's national bronco-riding champion! Girls, it *is* him. Oooh, I need your autograph. Sign here," she practically purred, and handed over a pen from her purse while pulling aside the V-neck of her shirt to expose the swell of her left breast.

Willow expected Coop to brush the loud women off, because their food had come up. But he didn't. Instead, he let them engulf him, and his laugh erupted like Mount Vesuvius. Willow watched his posture, wearing his winner's smile as he signed various body parts—although for the one in the V-neck, he only signed her arm. All the women gushed on and on about his stats. Time ticked by as their food cooled on the counter and the women continued fawning over Coop, talking rodeo.

Lily began to whimper, so Willow got up, marched across the restaurant and grabbed their tray before stalking back to their table.

Coop saw her and began extracting himself from the gaggle of fans. The quintet finally got the message and turned their attention to the order window once they saw their idol sit down with a woman and child.

Willow had opened Lily's package of chicken strips and now coaxed her daughter to eat. It was hard to miss Coop's jovial attitude. She didn't want to be snarky, but sounded that way when she said, "Quite the photo opportunity. A rodeo cowboy and his groupies. It certainly doesn't look to me as if you *want* to leave the circuit."

Slow to come down from the adrenaline rush stoked by his followers, Coop had to admit fan enthusiasm was a big part of riding to the buzzer and piling up points in the standings. Fan adulation went with the territory. "I don't understand what's bugging you. Collecting autographs is harmless fun for avid rodeo-goers," he said. "I quit rodeo, but it wasn't all that long ago. Hardcore fans still remember me."

Willow took his lack of concern as disregard of her. "The fact that you get your jollies letting bimbos paw you means nothing to me, Coop. Nothing at all!" She bit into her burger, refusing to look at him.

He frowned. Things he wanted to say crowded the tip of his tongue as all their old arguments about the rodeo poured back into his mind. He reined in his temper for Lily's sake. It made for a tense, quiet meal, and an even tenser drive to the Laundromat, where he went in alone to collect his clothes. The situation didn't improve on the trip back.

Chapter Six

Halfway to the ranch Coop wanted to break their silence in the worst way. It wasn't just that Willow was freezing him out by ignoring him. He'd begun to feel bad about participating in the juvenile antics back at the restaurant. He understood how it probably looked to a nonrodeo bystander. Those fans *were* kind of over the top. Admittedly that was part of what he'd grown tired of, even though it went with the whooping and hollering of a rodeo aftermath when scores and buckles were handed out.

Plain and simple, Willow disliked rodeos. Period. Plus, she'd insinuated that Tate screwed around with other women during their marriage. That was disgusting. Coop had enjoyed sexual favors from select women along the circuit, but he was single. His dad had drilled into him and Sully that it was okay to sow wild oats before a man committed to one woman in marriage. But Matt Drummond had loved his wife beyond his till-death-do-us-part vow. Coop had never seen his father look at, or flirt with, another woman.

"I'm sorry, Willow," he said abruptly, but in all earnestness.

Stirring, she glanced at him in surprise. "For what? Shh, lower your voice. Lily's asleep."

He took a peek over his shoulder. Sure enough, the girl's head lay propped against the generous wing of her new booster seat. She still clutched the disreputable-looking rabbit in the crook of one arm, but her face was softly relaxed. Her eyelashes curved like half-moons along pale, blue-veined cheeks. "She looks like an angel," he murmured as he forgot what he'd planned to apologize for.

Willow followed the line of Coop's sight. Her own lips slowly relaxed into a mother's loving smile. "I had so many hopes and dreams for her. I hate, hate, hate that I can't wave my hand and make her whole, make her well."

Coop swallowed a lump that didn't want to be dislodged from his throat. He never expected to feel so protective toward another man's child. Well, maybe toward his brother's son. But never Tate Walker's kid, especially considering the years of bad blood between them.

"I can see the way it's tearing you up, Willow."

She turned her face away to stare out the passenger window. "My heart breaks over and over. I have to pick up the pieces every time she falls apart and try to knit them back together again. Whatever the cause of her impairments, they're not her fault, and she deserves a mother who's strong enough to be her advocate."

"And you are," Coop said emphatically. He swung off the main road. The Ram bumped over the ruts carved into the gravel in front of Willow's house.

She didn't wait for him to round the hood and play

the gentleman. She hopped out and unbuckled Lily's seat belt, then headed to the house with the girl hoisted on her narrow shoulder before Coop had even cleared the front bumper.

"Do you need help?" he called out.

"Thanks, but no. I've got her. It's been a long day. It's past her bedtime. And mine," Willow said as she unlocked the door. "If you're still around tomorrow, we'll probably see you."

Coop stood for a moment, arms akimbo. *What the hell did she mean she'd see him if he was still around tomorrow?* Hadn't he just bought a power sprayer and ten gallons of paint? And didn't he have a fence to finish, plus a list of other chores?

Anger exploded in a red haze in front of his eyes then receded. A gold moon, the size of a beach ball, winked through the leafy oaks, and stars carpeted the night sky above, giving off enough light to unload the back of his pickup. Twinges of pain from his blistered palms reminded him of all the work he'd already done for Willow as he hauled the sprayer and paint cans to the side of her house.

He didn't know if he had it in him to keep batting at her objections to his help. He removed the booster seat from his pickup and strapped it into the rusted old Chevy Willow drove. The dash had cracked from the sun, and her vinyl seats were torn, with stuffing exposed in several spots. Was the damned thing even safe for her and Lily? he wondered, kicking at a tire to see if it held enough air. Worrying about them could drive him crazy. He retrieved the box that held his clean laundry and scuffed rocks out of his path on his way to the barn. He fed his horses and checked on the cattle, letting the cooling night breeze soothe his nerves as he hung his damp laundry over the stalls to dry. Too keyed up to go to bed, he dug out the magazines he'd bought earlier and read both articles on autism before he turned in for the night.

Tomorrow was another day, he thought as he stripped and settled down on his sleeping bag.

WILLOW HAD TOLD Cooper she was going to bed. She felt on edge and wasn't in the least sleepy. She didn't know what had made her go off on Coop like a shrew. She'd claimed that how he acted or with whom was none of her business, which was true. But, it hurt all the same, darn it.

Imbued with restless energy, she brewed a cup of herbal tea, then went into cleaning mode. It was her way of coping when she couldn't sleep or had problems on her mind. Willow scrubbed the floors, straightened the cupboards and polished the counters. Her thoughts wandered and she faced the fact that she kept telling Coop to go away, all the while wanting him to stay.

After her little fit today he'd probably decide she wasn't worth the effort. And really, was she? She'd let her tea go cold, so she reheated the water and plopped in a new tea bag. Idly stirring in a spoon full of honey, she mentally drew up a list of pros and cons, trying to view the situation from Coop's perspective.

To her discomfort, she couldn't come up with one thing about herself that he'd put in a pro column. He'd come here innocently, or so he swore, expecting to be hired for a few days by some woman in need of ranch help. What did he find? Her. That was like his past rising up to mock him. She and her ranch were in worse than poor shape. She lacked the tools with which to make repairs and then didn't even serve decent food to a hardworking man. The lineup of cons lengthened. Add to it the fact that, after he'd shelled out *his* money on her and Lily, she'd given him a tongue-lashing for something over which he had no control.

But that was what bothered her—he could have politely walked away from those women. It was embarrassing, watching him sign their bodies. And what had he said? That it was harmless fun for fans to collect autographs? On pieces of paper. Oh, why was she blaming them? Coop was nothing short of gorgeous. He had those long, lean muscles women loved. And that cowboy walk. Few women could pass up a second look if a real cowboy sauntered by. And with Coop, part of the package was his curly brown hair and coffee-colored eyes.... He was a man women wanted. Willow should know; *she'd* wanted him. But she'd given him up because of her fears, which at the time had been more consuming than her love for him.

Returning to the sink, Willow dumped her barely touched second cup of tea. Their pasts didn't matter now. Both of their lives had taken so many twists and turns, it would be too difficult to right old wrongs.

Exhausted from the long, traumatic day, she got ready for bed. It remained to be seen if Coop would pack up and head down the road before dawn.

THE FOLLOWING MORNING, she saw that his pickup was still parked next to the barn, so Willow set out his breakfast. She fed Lily and listened for Coop's tread on the porch. Hearing it at last, she held her breath and waited for him to knock and say he was leaving. The knock never came. Eventually she heard him ride out dragging the wooden sled he'd cobbled together the other day. Pulling aside the curtain, she saw that the sled was piled high with feed for the cattle.

She stifled her sigh of relief, then tried to ignore a surge of joy. He was free to stay or go. She'd managed okay since Tate's death. And she would continue to until a buyer showed up.

Just because Coop gave her another day's work didn't mean she could dawdle around. She'd pull her weight. He'd said the whole house needed to be power-washed before it could be painted. That sounded simple enough. If she did that herself, maybe Coop would have time to fix the underpinnings of the porch. She'd examined the rotten timbers in that corner, and repairing it was beyond her.

Willow opened the boxes holding the pieces of the power sprayer and took out the directions. She spread a blanket under the shade tree and gave Lily the three empty boxes to play with. Assembling the contraption took time, but it went together without a problem. Willow congratulated herself for not having any parts left over. Satisfied, she connected the hose to the back faucet, watched the unit fill, then turned it on. The force knocked her sideways. She tried to hang on, but the hose bucked and danced around like an angry snake. It spun in her hands and turned back on her, drenching her face, hair and clothing. "Yikes! Oh, yikes," she yelped as the now-slick hose jerked out of her grasp and began bouncing about, spraying everything but the house. She cried out again, dived after it, caught hold and, thinking she was turning the sprayer off, actually kicked it up to the next level of pressure. Because she'd aimed the nozzle at the siding, the power of the water blew her backward. Her feet flew out and she landed in the mud. She scrambled to her knees, all the while yelling at the contraption.

Coop heard her. He mounted up, tore down the hill and across the yard. Leaping off the horse, he grabbed the wildly swinging sprayer head and wrenched the faucet to the off position.

"Are you okay? Are you hurt?" he shouted, extending a hand to Willow, who still sat mired in water and mud.

Lilybelle dropped the biggest box and toddled toward her mother, dragging her rabbit. Not wanting her to get mud all over her favorite toy, Coop flung aside the sprayer and scooped up Lily. She didn't cry as he feared she would.

It took him a minute to figure out Willow wasn't shaking from tears, but instead she was laughing—so hard she held her sides with mud-streaked arms.

She tried to get up, but slipped to her knees again. Coop gingerly set the child down in a dry spot, and then helped Willow out of the muck. "I heard you yelling like a banshee. It scared the hell out of me," he said. "I'm glad to see you're not hurt, but I'll be darned if I see the humor in wallowing in a mudhole at 7:00 a.m."

Still holding her sides, acting on the spur of the moment, Willow plastered both muddy hands on Coop's chest, streaking his clean shirt. "Now who's all uptight and too serious?" she asked, giggling like a schoolgirl.

"Hey," he said, "I just washed this shirt yesterday."

"Oh, Coop, if you'd seen the whole thing you'd laugh, too. I'm sure I could've gone on *America's Funniest Home Videos*. I swear it felt as if that sprayer was alive."

"In hindsight," he said, "it *was* kind of amusing. Or it would've been it you hadn't yelled like you were being attacked."

"Sorry, it felt like I *was* being attacked. And here I was trying to be so helpful," she lamented, holding her mud-covered arms out from her equally muddy sides while she inspected the damage.

"If I'd known you were going to use the sprayer I wouldn't have bought the most powerful one they had. It's a commercial unit designed to spray with enough force to dislodge moss in the grooves of the siding. To use it full force, you need to stand farther away from the house."

"I figured that out, but then I couldn't shut it off and I couldn't hang on. Heavens, I'm a mess. I'll go clean up and try again."

"In the meantime, I'll do the back wall. Hey," he said. "Did you notice Lily B let me pick her up without making a fuss?"

"I missed that. I didn't know she'd left the boxes. She loves boxes. She can put her toy rabbit in a box and remove him a thousand times without tiring of the game. It's another quirk of her autism."

"So, you're saying I shouldn't be heartened by the fact that she didn't kick and bawl?"

Sorrow flickered across Willow's face. "Bless you for wanting to interact with her, Coop. Fear is her usual reaction whenever she faces a new experience. I guess it means she's getting used to seeing you around here."

"I suppose so. The magazine article I read says there are activities that work on the neuropathways in the autistic child's brain. According to the doctor who wrote it, some kids can make marked progress in areas of speech, cognition and facial expression."

"Oh, I hope so. That's why I'm praying for a buyer to drop into my lap."

"Well, I have about fifty more fence posts to set, the cattle are chowing down, adding weight every day, and if the siding dries quickly, we can paint soon. Then you can call your Realtor to come take another gander at the place. It might sell quicker if you'd lower your price."

"After I deduct what I owe you from the sale of steers and the property, Coop, I hope there'll be enough left for me to move somewhere I can find a good-paying job and a school for Lily. A day school. Not the boarding type."

"I don't recall asking to be paid back."

"I wouldn't feel right taking so much money from you." She held up a hand when Coop opened his mouth to argue again. "I need to go clean up. We'll hash this out later. You've spent the money already, but please don't spend any more," she said, glancing at Lily, who was back playing with her boxes.

Coop cranked up the sprayer after Willow shut the back door. He wondered how he'd feel in her place. Having a history such as theirs probably made accepting favors from him more difficult. He examined his motives for shelling out substantial bucks on her. He was depleting his bank account, but he couldn't quite explain why. He only knew he couldn't walk away and leave Willow and her child when they needed so much help.

He'd finished washing the back of the house by the time she emerged again. She looked fresh and scrubbed, and he thought her eyes had fewer worry lines around them than they had the first day he'd come upon her chasing those wayward steers. He compared how appealing she was right now to the duded-up, expensively styled women at the restaurant yesterday. Clamping down on his back teeth, Coop motioned with the sprayer and showed her how to regulate the pressure with a dial on the water container.

"Oh, I saw that when I assembled the unit, but I figured the tank would fill faster if it was fully open."

"Well, if you've never operated one of these before, all the moving parts take some getting used to."

Willow's gaze strayed to the blanket. "Coop, where's Lily?"

"I don't know. She was there a minute ago." He pushed up his sunglasses and scanned the area beneath the tree where she'd been sitting. The boxes lay there, but both the girl and her rabbit were gone.

"Weren't you watching her?" Willow asked.

He frowned. "You didn't ask me to."

"I assumed you would." Willow's voice rose in panic as she whirled one way, then the other. "She never wanders off. But you're right. It's my fault." Willow ran around the corner of the house.

"It's no one's fault," Coop said, putting the sprayer

down before jogging to catch up. "She probably followed you inside."

"I didn't see her."

"Go look again. She could've gotten hot and thirsty."

Willow's eyes reflected nothing but fear. "Lily doesn't think like that, Cooper. I have to remind her about those kinds of basic wants and needs." She rushed up the back steps and hurried into the house.

Coop walked over to the trees. At first he worried that she might have gone into the woods, but the underbrush was thick and nothing looked disturbed. No twigs bent or broken. He turned as Willow ran back out.

"She's not inside." Alarm raised the volume of Willow's voice. "She's never gone off by herself. Oh, God, Coop, where could she be?"

"Did you check her favorite spot on the front porch? I'm sure I would've seen her if she went around past me. But she could've gone through the house."

"Yes, I did look there. Would you have noticed if she went toward the barn?" Willow shaded her eyes against the bright afternoon sun.

"Yes, and the same if she'd headed for the road."

"That leaves the meadow where you've been working on the fence," Willow said, breaking into a run.

"Hold on. Let's ride up there on Legend," Coop shouted. "We'll cover the ground faster."

"Okay, but hurry, please! The pond's on the way. And Lily has no fear of water." Willow's voice broke. "I wasn't gone ten minutes. She usually sits in one spot for hours."

He swung into the saddle and rode to where Willow

was charging up the hill. Coop leaned down, caught her around the waist and swung her up to sit in front of him. Touching his heels to the gelding, they trotted off.

"Go faster, will you?"

"The ground's full of gopher holes. It's too easy for a horse to break a leg. Anyway, if we go more slowly, we can both keep our eyes peeled. She was wearing a red shirt and orange pants, right? She should stand out from quite a distance."

"She'd wear that same outfit day in and day out if I'd let her."

"I've noticed she likes that shirt." Coop zigzagged the horse to cover more territory. "You need a dog. One trained to watch over Lily. A service dog."

"Like I need one more mouth to feed. Don't you buy her a dog, Cooper. Oh, where is she?" Willow twisted from side to side. "Could she have come this far? How long was she out of your sight?"

"I wish I knew. Damn, I should've grabbed my binoculars from the pickup."

"Coop!" Willow grabbed the saddle horn and glanced back at him, her color draining. "The herd is coming down to the pond for water. What if she accidentally crosses their path? She could be trampled!"

"Don't borrow trouble, Willow."

"Easy for you to say. She's not your daughter."

"Do you think that makes me care any less?" Even as the statement left his lips, Coop recognized that it was true.

Willow went still as Coop's arms tightened around her waist. Heat from his body surrounded her. It was comforting in a way she hadn't experienced in a long, long while.

"I didn't mean to insult you, Coop. All I meant was that mothers and their children share a special bond from birth. And...and I'm panicking."

"Me, too. I'm sure she was on the blanket when I went to shut off the water at the faucet. Then poof, you noticed she was gone. Willow, look! To your left. By that broken rail fence. Under the redbud tree. It's Lily. She's sitting in a patch of flowers nearly as high as her head."

"I see her!" Willow let out a low cry of heartfelt relief and struggled to get down from the horse.

Reining in, Coop swung down, reached up and lifted Willow to the ground. She slid the length of his body, and ever so briefly they clasped each other, sharing an instant of joy.

Coop came close to whooping and spinning her around. As he held her close he met her eyes and saw the questions flickering there. Questions about his hug and his body's automatic reaction. Those were questions Coop wasn't prepared to answer. He attributed his purely male response to the emotions involved in Lily's disappearance. Emotions they'd shared during the ride. Making more of it pushed things farther than they should go. He'd dismissed those old feelings years ago. Releasing her, Coop stepped back. "Go," he said gruffly. "Get her home. I'll steer the herd away, then work on the fence until suppertime."

"Sure. All right." Willow stumbled in her haste to not only reach Lily, but also hide the inappropriate response that had welled up in her unexpectedly. She knew better. Knew Coop didn't feel about her the way she'd always felt about him. She ran toward her daughter, deciding that any relationship with Cooper Drummond was just too complicated.

Reaching the child, Willow dropped to her knees. If only she could pour out her pent-up feelings by hugging her. But Lily didn't enjoy close contact. And she disliked being interrupted.

"Hiya, babe." Willow sat back and let her pounding heart slow as she joined her daughter in picking wildflowers. "You haven't the faintest idea that you scared your mama half to death. And Coop, too. His hide's not so tough when it comes to you." Willow glanced toward him and couldn't resist a half smile.

From across the field, Coop turned the milling herd to the upper end of the pond. His eyes strayed often to the pair seated amid the colorful flowers. Sunlight broke through branches of the redbud tree to form crowns of light around the two on the ground. The woman's blond hair was a pale cloud in the dancing light, while the child's shone with an almond-brown luster.

Coop's stomach tensed when he saw Willow tilt back her head, her neck white and inviting. He thought he heard her laughter as she set a circle of flowers on Lily's curls.

An invisible hand seemed to grab his heart, squeezing it. How could Tate—how could any man—*not* feel privileged to have them as his family? Now that the worry for Lily's safety was over, Coop realized how frightened he'd been.

Cursing under his breath, he pulled on his gloves

and picked up a sledgehammer, what he felt for Willow and Tate Walker's daughter confused him. He would never have imagined he could feel such a connection to Tate's child. The next time he looked up, Willow and Lily were gone and the sun dipped low in the west, streaking the horizon with the same gold that reminded him of Willow's hair.

He'd hammered out most of his anxieties by afternoon's end. He hadn't fully reconciled all his confusion, but maybe he'd stepped over the hard line he thought he'd drawn to separate him from the old feelings he'd held for Willow. He began to head downhill so he could clean up for supper. Maybe it was time to test his rekindled interest in the lady of the house.

AFTER FILLING HIS BELLY, Coop took out his guitar. He was feeling a lot more mellow and his mood led him to play a series of love songs. He heard the screen door open and stopped strumming "Dream a Little Dream of Me." Cooper expected to see Willow, but it was Lily watching him. He continued to play and she edged nearer as he softened the chords. A moment later she set her hand on his knee and cocked her head as if to absorb the sound. Afraid to break the spell he nevertheless changed tempo. She seemed to like the more energetic beat; her eyes brightened, and Coop saw the corners of her lips curve up in a smile. It was the first time he'd seen any change in her expression, and he got so excited, he forgot to play.

From inside, Willow called out for Lily. She burst through the door and grabbed the girl. "There you are, honey bunny," she exclaimed, relief in her shaky voice.

"Willow." Coop caught her hand. "Lily came out to listen to my music. She walked right up and put her hand on my knee and then…she smiled."

"Cooper, stop it. I know I accused you of allowing her to run off and I'm sorry. But there's no need to make up stories to appease me. I'm well aware that Lily doesn't react to what goes on around her. And what happened today reinforces that I need to be even more vigilant and not let her out of my sight."

Coop put his guitar back in its case. He heard Willow's pain, and because of that he made an effort to sound reasonable. "Why would I lie to you, Willow? I swear Lily likes music. And…maybe she likes me," he said, feeling a little defensive. However, he might as well have been talking to the wind. Willow went into the house, shutting the door, shutting him out.

Chapter Seven

Uneasy about the way they'd left things the night
before, Coop—who usually plunged whole-hog into
every endeavor—decided to take this slower, this ex-
ploration of his one-time relationship with Willow. The
relationship prior to their series of bitter arguments
over his chosen career and her subsequent defection
to Tate Walker. She could have picked any other man
of Cooper's acquaintance and Coop would be able to
forgive and forget. But Tate had been a burr under his
saddle from the day Bart Walker bought the land bordering the Drummond ranch, and the boys, both eight
at the time, squared off across a roan mare Coop had
raised from a filly. It'd been his first real love affair
with a horse, and Tate was climbing onto the roan. It
was clear to Coop that his neighbor planned to steal the
horse Coop hadn't branded yet because he couldn't bear
to mar her beautiful, dark red coat.

Tate first claimed he was returning the horse, saying
he found her running loose on his dad's property. But
Coop knew a fence that had been separated with wire
cutters when he saw one. He knew a thief when he
looked one in the eyes. And he knew a brazen lie when
he heard it. In Coop's estimation, Tate had never re-

formed and the two had a chilly association from that day forward. How could Willow not have known that, since she was so often at the center of later animosity? Maybe she *had* been clueless, given how busy and absorbed she always was.

Instead of slamming the door against any and all conversation concerning Tate, he should've asked her why she'd married the jerk. Another woman might have deliberately married his nemesis to cause maximum hurt to the guy who didn't do what she wanted. Willow wasn't like that. Cruelty wasn't in her DNA.

All of the thoughts that had been rocketing through Coop's head continued as he stripped and hosed down at the end of what had been another arduous workday.

Clean and refreshed, he slung his guitar case over his back and followed his nose across the yard to the porch. It was obvious Willow was cooking supper.

The shadier front of the house hadn't yet dried from the power washing Willow had done that day, so he couldn't take his usual spot on the top step. Nothing had been returned to the porch, including the orange crate where Willow placed his meals. Or maybe she was still annoyed at him and had decided not to feed him tonight.

Coop contemplated their previous day. If she *was* mad at him, he was probably to blame. As he debated whether or not to knock, the screen door flew open and Willow backed out carrying one of her kitchen chairs. He was unable to get out of her way fast enough, and she crashed into him.

"Oof! Coop, I didn't see you. Why were you sneaking up behind me?" Willow lost her purchase on the chair; together they lunged for it as the chair spun and tilted, nearly toppling them both. Coop grabbed a post and saved them from falling off the porch.

"If that chair is meant for me, wouldn't it be easier if I just come inside and ate at your kitchen table?"

"You know my rules, Coop."

"They'd make sense if your hired hand was a stranger. Don't you trust me?"

"It's not a matter of trust. I told you Lily is a picky eater. She might not eat at all if I disrupted her routine."

"That's bogus. She ate chicken strips at the restaurant and we all sat at the same table. And last evening she smiled at me whether you choose to believe it or not."

Willow rolled her eyes. "The chair is here, and I have your plate ready," she said, obviously not budging, because she hurried into the house again.

Coop rested his guitar case against the porch railing and moved the chair around until he found a flat spot.

"I saw you making daisy chains with Lily yesterday after we found her," Coop said the minute Willow returned with his covered plate. "For all the worry she caused us, I…well, I know it's not for me to say, but how does making playtime out of a bad situation teach her it's wrong to wander off like she did?"

"Are you suggesting I should have spanked her or something?"

"Of course not! I'd never advocate hitting a kid. But wasn't it a situation where child experts would recommend a time-out? I've only seen them interviewed on TV programs, mind you," he said to keep Willow from asking what made him an authority, as she was plainly about to do.

She crossed her arms. "Normal rules for raising children don't apply to kids with autism. Experience has taught me that if Lily senses my displeasure, it can cause a meltdown. You haven't witnessed one of those. Someone who didn't know her condition might call it a tantrum. Meltdowns are more than tantrums. They can go on until she wears out. And, in the end, there's no understanding on her part. She doesn't realize how she screamed and carried on. A book I bought says it's a lack of deductive reasoning. She has a brain disorder, Cooper."

"I know that. I'm trying to understand."

"So am I. Sorry if I get my hackles up. I want to help her so badly, and it kills me that I don't know how." She gestured to the plate he still held. "You'd better eat before your pot roast gets cold."

"Ah, that's what I smelled. You should go on in and eat, too. But can I borrow the book you mentioned?"

Willow shrugged. "There's a lot of technical jargon to wade through. I don't know why you'd want to read it. I mean, you'll be leaving in a day or two."

Well, that hurt. Coop tried not to show it. "I didn't pick up any more reading material on our last trip to town. Besides, I may be here longer than a day or two. It'll take three to finish the fence, and I haven't had a chance to call around and see which trucking outfit will give us the best price to take your steers to the stockyard. Or have you made those calls?"

She shook her head. "I've never sold so many head a

one time. The feed-store owner always located buyers for one or two steers and the buyers came here."

"It doesn't work that way when you unload a whole herd. Don't worry, Willow. I'll try to call around tomorrow. In another week, they'll be fat enough to bring in top dollar, but they need to be vaccinated with booster antibiotics and branded before you sell them."

"I didn't realize that. I guess I'm not a very good rancher." She went inside then, but her comment made Coop wonder about what Willow planned to do after she sold her herd. Ideally selling the cattle would coincide with selling the ranch. But how would she manage if the ranch didn't sell right away? Hanging on to the place would drain all the proceeds from the beef sale. If Coop could find time to work with the mare and colt he'd seen, they could bring in some ready cash. The horses weren't wild, but they weren't tame, either. And the mare wasn't branded. The colt had good lines. If he was going back to the Triple D after he left here, he'd want to start breeding horses again. A mare and her sturdy colt might be a good first acquisition. *If* he was going back to the Triple D. At some point he had to, if for no other reason than to clear the air between him and Sully.

Coop enjoyed every bite of Willow's savory pot roast, potatoes and carrots. He'd have enjoyed the meal more with company, but that was wishful thinking. He was a social person, and here, the long, empty hours of solitude were beginning to get to him. Coop supposed he'd face the same lonely existence if he moved home. Sullivan and Blythe both led busy lives. He'd probably have to move into the older house where he'd grown up. It was a house meant for a family.

Sobering at his own thoughts, Coop set his empty plate aside, took out his guitar and kicked back in the chair. He started in with a song that matched his feelings.

Willow came out and took his plate then went in again, quietly closing the screen door behind her.

Part way into a lullaby frequently used by cowboys to calm restless herds during roundups, Coop noticed that Lily had pushed open the screen. Freshly scrubbed, ready for bed, she held her rabbit by its ear and somberly watched him play.

Coop spoke softly to her. "You like music, Lily B? I think so. Can you say *music?* It's kind of a hard word. Mu..si..c," he said again, stretching out the syllables.

She slipped out and cautiously moved closer. Pleased, Coop segued from one song to another. He was running out of tunes he knew off the top of his head, so it was probably just as well that they both heard Willow calling Lily's name. The girl scampered back to the door, but her big, luminous eyes never left the guitar or Coop's hands.

"There you are, honey bun," Willow exclaimed. "After I cleaned the tub, I expected to find you and Mr. Rabbit snuggled down in bed." Stepping out onto the porch, her feet as bare as her daughter's, Willow picked up Lily and blew a raspberry on her neck. "How can I keep a more watchful eye on you kiddo, when you sneak off like this? My heart sinks whenever you aren't where I expect you to be."

"She came out to hear my music," Coop said. "You like music, don't you, Lily B?"

The child buried her face in her mother's shoulder, and Willow shook her head at Coop. "You are such an optimist. But I like your serenade," she told him.

"Are you coming back out?" Coop asked, strumming aimless chords.

Willow glanced around. "The porch is still wet. I thought it'd be dry by now."

"I can bring out another chair while you put Lily to bed."

"I don't know, Coop. We ate supper later than usual. I worked hard today. I should probably turn in, too."

"Hard work is all the more reason to wind down slowly. And I meant it earlier when I asked to borrow that book on autism."

"Oh, right. I forgot. I'll get it. Meanwhile, would you mind playing some of the old songs you guys played in college? Maybe 'Bridge Over Troubled Water'?"

"I'll see if I remember any of those tunes. Around the rodeo, everybody's into country music."

"Anything is okay, Coop. I miss the radio we had. It was one of the first things I sold to a drifter I hired to work here after Tate was killed."

She withdrew then, and Coop decided a radio was definitely something he'd buy for Willow before he left. She needed one for practical reasons. Texas was known for its erratic storms. He'd find a portable with a reliable antenna so she could use it outside.

He hauled out a second chair in hopes she'd change her mind. Picking up his guitar again, he strummed portions of songs he remembered from his college days.

Willow was gone longer than he thought she'd be, and he'd run through most of his repertoire before she appeared at the screen door again. Happy to see her, he stopped playing. It had grown so dark he had to hold the book she passed to him up to the light spilling from the house. *"Autism, the Invisible Disability,"* he read. "I promise I'll get it back to you soon."

"This covers a lot, but I know there are newer studies, and newer guides to coping, since I bought this book. Our library is minuscule. They don't have many medical books."

"They ought to be able to order what you want from the state system."

"Except that it was built through donations and is staffed by volunteers."

"You need access to the latest information. I never gave any thought before as to what a challenge disabilities must be for rural families."

"Why would you, unless you knew someone who's affected?" She moved about the porch, leaning on the railing, gazing up at the moon.

"It's none of my business," Coop said, clearing his throat. "And I realize I took your head off the other night for mentioning Tate. But considering what you did say, Willow, why didn't you leave with Lilybelle before it was too late? I mean, before the time Tate ran you off the road and dragged you back."

She sank down on the second chair and rubbed her hands across her face. "Fear, Coop. He said he'd track me down and see that Lily was taken away. I had no money of my own. I'm a college dropout. I knew Tate's dad wouldn't help me, because he made that plain before we got married. My mom couldn't. I decided that unless things got really bad here, at least we had food and a roof over our heads."

"What about the abuse?"

"Don't judge me, Cooper! Tate's abuse was mostly verbal. He hit me once, but if he'd ever hit Lilybelle, nothing would have kept me here."

Coop didn't bring up the fact that the owner of the feed store said his wife had observed bruises on Willow when she was pregnant. Arguing would serve no purpose. And he couldn't make a dead man pay. "How many credits are you short to graduate?" he asked instead. "You planned to be a teacher. I always thought you'd be a great one. And it's a job that would give you summers off with Lily."

"I left college my junior year. I didn't get credit for the semester of practice teaching I did because I left midterm. Do you think I haven't dreamed of going back to get my degree? But if and when I move from here, I need to get a job with benefits and a salary that'll cover rent, food, clothes and special schooling for Lilybelle."

Coop fiddled with the book jacket. "You should explore school options available for single moms. I'll bet there are loans and grants. This ranch is small, but it should still bring in enough to tide you over until you can finish your degree. And colleges sometimes have child-care programs on campus."

"Really? I've only expected to sell for enough to cover what's owed on the mortgage and buy the gas we'd need to get to San Antonio or Austin."

"I didn't know you owed on the ranch. The guy at

the feed store said Tate bragged about how his dad had set him up here. How much is left on the loan?"

"I'm not sure. Tate and his dad refinanced before Tate died. But all I've been paying is the interest. I told the Realtor I won't sell for less than I owe the bank." She closed her eyes and massaged the back of her neck.

Coop could see the conversation was stressing her. "Hey, I'm keeping you from bed." He stood, set the book on the railing and put his guitar back in its case. "I'll shore up this porch in the next few days."

"Saying thanks again doesn't seem like enough for everything you've done for me, Cooper."

"Well, it keeps me from going back to the Triple D and having to face Sully."

She studied him. "Your brother is a hard man."

"Yeah...well..." Coop shrugged as he lifted both chairs and prepared to take them inside.

"You don't want to leave one chair out here to use at breakfast?"

"Nah. Just pack me a few biscuits and some bacon. I'll make a few sandwiches to eat as I ride out to work on the fence. By the end of tomorrow, this wood should be dry enough to sit on again."

She held the door and waited until after he left the porch to lock up.

BEFORE RETIRING, Willow checked on Lilybelle, who lay on top of her covers, arms and legs splayed willy-nilly. *Such a sweet cherub in sleep.* Luckily, most of the time, she was sweet while awake, too. But Willow hadn't lied to Cooper. Sometimes, handling Lily's explosive behavior was a trial. Rescuing the rabbit from the floor, Willow tucked him under the blanket where Lily could easily see him when she woke up.

In her own room, Willow prepared for bed. But she found sleep elusive. Hopes and dreams she'd long ago put on the back burner flooded back, thanks to Coop's prodding. Yes, she still longed to be a teacher. Coop knew her current situation, yet he'd made her hope that finishing her degree might be possible.

Yawning, she turned on her side. That was one thing she used to love about Cooper. He always put the best spin on everything. But there was a downside, too. He refused to take her concerns about the rodeo seriously at a time when the very thought of him climbing into a chute day after day simply terrified her. She wadded her pillow under her head. All her worries had been for nothing. He'd emerged in one piece. And oh, what a piece. Willow fell asleep imagining how nice it would be to have Coop curled around her in bed.

THE NEXT MORNING, Cooper's day didn't start off well. He broke the handle off the sledgehammer, which put an end to driving fence posts. Taking a second look at the sagging porch, he discovered a leak in the kitchen plumbing; that was what had caused the support beam to rot out. He crawled under and found the pipe he needed to replace.

"Willow, I have to run into town to pick up a new handle for the sledgehammer and a few plumbing supplies. Do you need anything? Are we running low on milk or eggs?"

"The hens out back are laying again. Milk—we always need milk. I shouldn't have sold the milk cow, but the drought killed the sweet grass, and feeding her became an issue. Are you sure you want to mess with buying groceries when you're going after tools?"

"It's all at the same store. Make a list. I'll go check on how much grain I have left for my horses. I might as well get everything in one trip."

Willow propped her shoulder against the door frame and watched him walk away in that slow, hip-rolling gait she loved. She spared another second to marvel at him. Tate had never set foot in a grocery store to buy anything except beer.

She found a couple of things that needed replenishing. But then, after Coop drove off, she started to worry about the cost. He hadn't asked for money, and she hadn't given him any from her emergency stash. From long habit, she kept enough hidden in her tampon box to buy bus tickets for her and Lily. That was the one place she knew Tate would never search even when he was drunk and tearing through the house looking for cash to spend on booze or cards. She probably should hand the money over to Coop, but although her situation had changed, it was still difficult to relinquish her means of escape.

WILLOW HAD PREPARED chicken-fried steak and fries, which were warming in the oven when Coop finally drove in. She exhaled and dropped the window curtain. He'd been gone so long her stomach was a jumble. Logic said he wouldn't leave without his horses. Logic said he wouldn't go on a bender as Tate so often did. Logic didn't say Coop wouldn't hook up with some woman in town, though.

While she dished up a second helping of macaroni and cheese for Lily, Willow took deep breaths to calm her frayed nerves.

She didn't expect Coop to barge right into the house, laden down with more groceries than had been on her list.

"Whatever you're cooking smells good." He sniffed the air as he divested himself of sacks and stowed the milk in the fridge. "Oh, it's ready," he noted as Willow removed two covered plates from the oven. "Let's eat at your table, then I'll put away the rest of this stuff. Sorry I'm late. I had to go to Crystal City for the plumbing supplies. Carrizo Springs was having a parade and a chile festival by the time I arrived back there for groceries. You and Lily are probably the only people in this area who weren't there. Traffic was at a standstill." Without waiting for her to insist he eat on the porch, Coop washed up at the kitchen sink, and relieved her of one of the warm plates she still held in her oven mitts.

He sat and tucked right into his food.

Willow opened her mouth to protest his high-handedness, first casting a sidelong glance at Lily-belle, who kept spooning in her food. Seeing that her daughter had no concerns, and since she didn't want to seem ungrateful Willow sat down, took off the mitts and slowly peeled the foil off her plate. "I didn't know about the festival. I don't bother with the local paper. I never found time to read it."

"I bought you a radio," Coop said.

That stopped Willow. "You what? Cooper! Radios are expensive!"

"It's a gift. And don't be selling it, either. You

need to know what's going on around here, and in the world."

"I… Thank you. I don't know what else to say."

"That's sufficient. It's not a big deal."

But it was to Willow. Bigger than he knew.

No further talk passed between them as they ate. The silence wasn't uncomfortable, though. Willow reflected that she shouldn't have balked at letting him eat with them before.

They finished about the same time and she cleared the table. She put their dishes in the sink to soak, then turned to help him unload the sacks still sitting on the counter. "What's this?" she asked, removing a smaller plastic bag from the sack that held a box of cereal.

"A coloring book and crayons for Miss Lily," Coop said, smiling at the little girl. "It's a book of farm animals. The crayons are nontoxic."

"Coop…"

"You keep saying my name in that tone that suggests you think I'm an idiot."

"No. Never that." She swallowed all the emotions threatening to choke her. "I already tried coloring with her, but she ate the crayons. I'm…touched by your generosity, and at a loss for words.

"I'm not looking for thanks." He leafed through the coloring book and tore out a page with a pony on it. "Po…ny," he said repeatedly. "Po…ony." He pointed to the picture he'd placed in front of Lily. Then he sat adjacent to her and dumped out the fat crayons. Selecting the red one, he said, "Red. The color of your shirt." He pointed. "Blue, the color of my shirt." Coop made each association, then ran the crayon across the pony's body.

"Now you do it," he said, pleased to see her bend for a closer look. He fit her fingers around the crayon but she pulled back and dropped it. Again Coop colored, and again handed her the crayon. This time she took it and scribbled on the picture, then kept coloring.

Fascinated by his patience, Willow put away the rest of the groceries. She found the radio. Coop's buying it had been more than thoughtful. But she was far more touched by his purchase of a simple coloring book. To see her daughter actually take the crayon and scribble on the drawing of a horse filled her heart with an uncommon happiness. Did Coop know his act of kindness toward Lilybelle meant even more to her than all the backbreaking work he'd done around her ranch? She doubted it. She wanted to hug him. That would be unwise; there was still a wall of reserve between them.

Coop raised his head, caught Willow watching him intently, and his lips moved in a slow smile.

Unable to respond with the words of love that tangled her tongue, Willow released a pent-up breath. "Cooper Drummond," she murmured, "You are such a kid."

He winked, his smile lasting until Lily tired of running colors across the rainbow-hued pony. She sat back, hugged her rabbit and fought to keep her eyes open while Coop boxed up the crayons.

Willow noticed. "It's bedtime for you, young lady." Coming around the counter, she scooped up her sleepy daughter. "Coop... I..."

He stood. "It's late. I'll let myself out," he said, stacking the crayons on top of the coloring book. He and Willow were both speechless when Lily twisted in her mother's arms, stretched out a hand and nabbed the page she'd colored.

They didn't need to comment on the girl's momentous action. The knowledge that it spelled some kind of a change in their strained relationship was reflected in two pairs of eyes that met over Lily's head.

Chapter Eight

The next few days marched past in four-four time. Willow worked on painting the house while Coop finished the fence. One afternoon, he mentioned needing Liquamycin to vaccinate the herd.

"Is that really necessary? How costly would that be?"

"I told you it's needed to sell them. I'll do it myself and save getting a vet out here. That's where the biggest cost would be."

"That's nice of you, Coop. But isn't it too much work?"

"I'm fine with it, Willow."

The morning Coop decided to go into town after the vaccine, he stopped at the house first. Willow was already painting. She'd started on the shady side of the house as it'd been so hot. Coop thought she looked cute in shorts and her too-big gloves. With her blond hair tied up in loopy braids, she reminded him a little of Daisy Duke.

She bobbed her head in time to music blaring from the radio, and Lily sat on a blanket near the radio, too. He was glad she liked his gift, and made a mental note to stock up on batteries. Still, the idea of leaving her on the ranch alone gave him pause. "Hey, I'm going into town. Do you need anything?"

Willow hadn't seen him, and jumped when he spoke behind her.

"I did a count, and over half your herd aren't branded," he added. "I don't want you to get cheated at market. Counting brands is the only way to safeguard against that. But I can't find a branding iron in the barn or shed. You couldn't have sold something so specific. Do you know where the irons might be?"

"The yearlings were born about the time Tate died. Bart didn't come to the ranch, but he sent a vet to give the calves something Bart called their five-in-one shots. None of them were branded, but those wouldn't represent half my herd. Steers over a year old, Tate should have branded."

Big surprise, Coop thought. Another job Tate had skipped. "Tate was all about show and no substance. If he lacked the skill to prove he was the best at anything, he didn't tackle the job, or he lied to cover up his inadequacies. He fooled a lot of people," Coop muttered. It still grated to think Willow hadn't seen through the lazy bum.

She stood there, paint dripping from her brush, her blue eyes suddenly hard. "I'm sorry another one of my problems has been dropped in your lap, Cooper."

He slashed a hand through the air. "Do you have a registered brand?"

"Wouldn't my brand be what's on the older cattle? *Now* what's wrong?" she demanded as Coop pursed his lips. "You look like you ate a lemon."

"Your older cows have the Bar W, Bart Walker's

brand. Considering all the claims Sully's filed against him for rustling, I'm not keen to try and sell Bar W cows at a major market."

Willow drew in a sharp breath, then shifted her gaze to her daughter, rocking on her blanket. "Lilybelle and I *are* Walkers," she said emphatically. "If you'll brand my cattle, *I* will sell them at market. No need for you to bother yourself."

Coop removed his hat and slapped it against his thigh three or four times as anger at her words sizzled inside him. "Thunderheads are building in the south. We may be in for a storm. So we should keep our eyes peeled for signs the next few afternoons." With a brief, jerky nod, he resettled his hat on his sweaty head, wheeled around on a worn boot heel, walked to his pickup and climbed in.

The dust kicked up by his oversize tires had blown past before Willow was able to resume her painting. Here she thought they'd gotten past the hurdle of Tate, but obviously not. Even though she'd made a real effort... After the night with the coloring, she'd invited Coop to have supper in the house with her and Lily.

Now she wasn't sure it was such a good idea—for *her* sake. Lily was thriving. In the nights since that first coloring episode, she'd filled half the pages of the book with her earnest scribbles. She loved the pony best. She carried the page around, but remained mute whenever Coop told her the name of each color, repeating them over and over. Lily could actually pick out red, blue and yellow, her favorite crayons, as Cooper named them, which delighted Willow. And Lily showed a definite preference for the bright ones. She refused to use black or brown. Coop seemed to think that was significant. What each small step did was give Willow renewed hope and confirm the need to move someplace where she'd be able to find an appropriate school for her daughter.

If Willow had been lulled into believing her relationship with Coop had improved, the branding discussion dashed her hopes. And Coop was in town all day. It was well past suppertime when he returned, and then he went straight to the barn after unloading whatever he'd bought. The plate of spaghetti and meatballs she'd kept warm for him in the oven dried out. It felt as if her heart shriveled a bit, too, like the overcooked spaghetti.

That night she couldn't help herself; she soaked her pillow with her tears. Crying was something she hadn't done in months. Crying weakened her and solved nothing. Coop couldn't know how many tears she'd shed over him in the years since he'd gone off to rodeo. Oh, how she regretted letting him go.

The one bright spot in her marriage had been the birth of her baby. And that joy had only lasted until Lily's diagnosis.

Coop might hate the Walkers, but the Drummonds had their faults, as well. Sullivan wasn't exactly a charmer. Willow blotted her tears, recalling an altercation she'd had with Sully Drummond shortly before she and Tate left Hondo. Cooper's brother blamed her for Coop's going off to rodeo. As if she had the power to stop him! Would Sully care that she'd paid again and again for marrying Tate?

He probably hadn't given her another thought after

ranting at her that day. Coop's brother and Tate's dad were both rich, powerful, difficult men. Tate took delight in telling her that Sully ran the Triple D with an iron fist and that he hated her for not stopping his little brother from leaving Hondo. Then Tate would laugh. And Bart Walker clearly thought his son was stupid to marry, "a Drummond's leavings." Of course, Tate's dad judged all women by his kids' mother, who'd run off, abandoning him and his two sons.

Climbing out of bed, Willow blew her nose and washed her tear-swollen eyes with cool water. She could imagine what Coop's brother would have to say now if he suspected her of trying to worm her way back into Coop's life. According to Tate, Sully had married a veterinarian. A smart, classy, professional woman. They were older by half a dozen years, and Willow hadn't spent any time at the Triple D, because her mother hadn't thought it was "proper" for a girl to visit a ranch run by three men. So she knew virtually nothing about Sully's wife. Her world back then had been narrow. She'd attended school, worked part-time stocking grocery shelves at night and helped her mother take care of her dad.

She crawled back into bed, but couldn't stop reviewing the past. She doubted Sully or anyone would believe she'd married Tate because she loved Cooper too much. But it was true. She loved him too much to risk marriage, certain she couldn't be the wife he'd need if he had an accident or was maimed for life on the circuit. She already experienced what being a rodeo invalid had done to her father—and her family. She was positive she didn't have what it would take to see Cooper killed or maimed by being thrown off a bucking horse. That fear, especially the fear that he might die, had paralyzed her.

Men as strong and tough as Sully Drummond wouldn't understand the toll her father's accident took on her and her mom. Yet people had seen them cope, so they'd probably find her intense fear for Coop hard to believe—and the fact that it had driven her to accept Tate's marriage proposal even harder. During Sully's rant, he'd told her everybody in Hondo knew Tate coveted everything Coop had.

Not her. She hadn't been so naive as to suppose Coop and Tate's many run-ins had nothing to do with her. But once she'd made her choice to marry Tate, she thought all of them—Sully, Cooper and Tate himself—should have known she'd never be a disloyal wife.

However, the ink on her marriage certificate was barely dry when Tate boasted about beating Coop in this one area that would hit Coop the hardest—like she was a trophy in a sporting match. Unfortunately, during unpacking, Tate had found and read an old diary of hers. In it, like the silly high school girl she'd been, she'd written that she'd always love Coop Drummond.

That had infuriated Tate. From then on, he'd isolated her here on the ranch as much as possible, and he'd punished her by making sure she saw every rodeo magazine that showed Coop with a bevy of women.

Pride stopped her from leaving Tate that first year before Lilybelle was born. She'd mistakenly assumed her pregnancy would effect a change in her husband's conduct toward her. It hadn't.

Flopping over, Willow kicked off the sheet. Yes,

she'd been foolish back then, but now her focus had to be on Lily—on securing better medical assessments and schooling. As much as she'd love to explain her situation so Coop could understand it, she couldn't, no matter how desperately she long to have him back in her life.

THE NEXT MORNING, after suffering a restless, sleepless night, Willow resolved to do what she had to about Coop. Determined to end his stay on her ranch, she drove the old pickup, with Lily in her booster seat, out onto the range.

Early though it was, the sun was already beating down and Coop worked without his shirt. Stopping by the new fence he'd installed, Willow watched him rope, throw and quickly vaccinate a bawling steer. The play of Cooper's tanned muscles as he performed his task was like a kick to her stomach. She remembered how smooth yet hard his body had once felt under her exploring hands. Looking at him now reminded her how long it'd been since she'd had enjoyable sex.

Mouth dry, she clambered out of the aging Chevy and hauled Lily into her arms.

Coop had cut out another huge Angus steer when he noticed Willow climbing onto the fence. "What's up?" he asked, trotting over to meet her. "You and the kiddo shouldn't be inside the enclosure. The shots can make the cattle cantankerous."

Willow backed away, but against her will, her eyes were drawn to the wings of dark hair that dusted his pecs, trailing down in a narrow ribbon to his navel, then disappearing under one of his flashy championship belt buckles. "I was going to tell you last night, Coop, but you didn't come to the house for supper. I just can't accept your charity anymore. This time it's not open for negotiation. You have to leave. Tomorrow at the latest."

Frowning, Coop walked to a tree and picked up a thermos, pouring water over his head before taking a swallow. His back ached. He was sunburned to a crisp, and parched. Yesterday he'd had to drive all the way to Eagle Pass, a border town, to find a vet clinic that could supply him with enough syringes to vaccinate Willow's herd. Vaccination that should've been done by Willow's lazy, good-for-nothing husband. How was he supposed to react to the news that she was kicking him off her ranch?

Having delivered her message, Willow set Lily outside the fence and then began to climb over. She'd hardly had a leg up when Coop reached across the fence and circled her upper arm. "Wait a darned minute. I thought we had a plan. I'm only half-done vaccinating. I had a blacksmith make up an iron yesterday so that once I'm finished with this I can begin branding. Am I happy about using the Bar W? Hell, no. But they're your cows, and I'm just the hired hand. I figured we went back far enough that I could tell you how I felt about Bart Walker without you getting into a snit." He paused. "I'm assuming our discussion about brands yesterday is the catalyst for your little speech today."

She shook loose from his grasp, but even then felt the imprint of his fingers on her arm. "The real crux of the matter is that you're not just my hired hand. The more you take on, the more you do around here, the more I owe you. I don't like being indebted to anyone. And you made quite clear yesterday how little you really think of me—of my choices at least."

"Bullshit," he lashed out. He would've said more, but Willow reared back and her eyes grew stormy.

"Ears," she hissed, cupping her palms over Lily's small ears.

"Sorry," Coop shot back with a modicum of guilt. "Oh, what the hell. Why should I fight to stay someplace I'm not wanted?"

Willow clenched her hands at her sides, but it rocked her to hear Coop state that so bluntly. Still faced off, their attention was drawn down hill to the main highway, where a dark-colored SUV with smoked windows passed slowly. When the vehicle reached the end of Willow's property, instead of speeding up to go on, the driver swung out, made a U-turn and went back the way he'd come, moving even more slowly.

"Anyone you recognize?" Coop asked Willow.

She shook her head. "Maybe it's one of your rodeo groupies trying to track you down."

"Why don't you cut me some slack," he snapped. "It's more likely a prospective buyer sent here by your Realtor to have a look."

"You think so?" she asked excitedly. Then her tension returned. "I should be down there painting the front of the house instead of arguing with you."

"Take it easy. They would've seen the paint cans and the ladder, and they would've noticed that one side is already a different color."

"I hope so. Having the siding washed and the porch

and fence repaired makes it look a lot better. I should get back down there and start on the front."

"I'll finish up here today, then come and help you," Coop said, as if she hadn't just fired him.

She scooped up Lily, who was a foot or so away, absorbed in picking dandelions. Boosting the girl onto her hip, Willow was shocked when her daughter twisted in her arms and extended the flowers she held toward Cooper. She said a word that sounded a lot like *music.*

Coop leaned over the fence and took the flowers. "Did you hear that, Willow? Now do you think you can admit that maybe I was right about the smile, right about her getting something out of my playing?"

Tears filled Willow's eyes as she hugged her daughter. "Yes, yes," she said shakily.

"Why are you crying? It's a solid breakthrough. We need to build on her interest in my guitar. I'll go into town and buy her an electronic keyboard. We can set it up in her room and show her how to pound on it and make music for herself." His gestures demonstrated his excitement. "There's no reason for me not to stay on, Willow."

"But there is," she said, remaining firm. "I'm grateful for everything you've done, Cooper. I am. But I can't afford to let Lily get too attached to you. You can't stay." Willow hurried to her pickup, sheltering the child in her arms as if any exposure to Coop now would be harmful.

He scowled after her, thinking none of her recent actions made any sense. Just this morning he'd texted Sully, asking his brother to transfer some funds into his nearly depleted bank account. Coop had stuck his neck out, telling Sully where he was. He'd explained how he'd stumbled across Willow, said Tate was dead and that Willow needed his help.

Sullivan had texted back, giving Coop hell, asking what kind of idiot he was. He'd let Willow humiliate him once by marrying their jerk of a neighbor, and now Coop wanted Triple D profits to do—what? Prove he was a better man than that useless Tate Walker? Sully had said Coop was off his rocker. And in typical big-brother fashion, he'd ordered Coop home to do his share of work on the ranch and maybe earn some part of what he'd cavalierly considered his due.

Coop was still steamed. He owned one half the damned ranch! Coming out here to work out his anger roping and throwing these bad-boy steers suited his mood. Mad at Sully, and feeling no benevolence toward Willow at the moment, Coop threw his back into finishing the chore he'd started.

The way he'd left things with Sully, Coop figured he had no alternative other than to waste a whole day driving to the Triple D to duke it out face-to-face. Sully could fork over some money as a loan against future work, or he could buy out Coop's interest in the ranch. If Sully had to mortgage his ass to do that, it'd serve him right.

Coop roped five more uncooperative steers and gave them shots. Sweat poured off him and was breathing hard. His exertion diminished his fury. Finally able to examine the situation more objectively, he considered what wasting a couple of days to make the round trip drive home might mean. If that was a prospective buyer in the SUV, Willow could sign a deal and just take off.

Then he might never find her again if, say, she went to one of the bigger cities she'd mentioned that offered better care for Lilybelle. Especially if she *wanted* to disappear, if she didn't want him to locate her.

Coop couldn't say why that very notion cut him so deeply, but it did.

The problem with doing a mindless task like this, no matter how physical, was that it let his thoughts run rampant.

Pushing himself to finish the last thirty head or so, Coop began to realize how much he liked having Willow in his life again. And Lily, named for his mother. That sweet child was a bonus.

He spent another hour mulling over this revelation. Draining his thermos of water, Coop stopped short of calling his still-conflicted feelings for Willow *love*. But...

His hastily thrown rope missed a steer zigzagging through stickery mesquite. A branch slapped back, ripping a welt along his side, which sprouted a few drops of blood. That made him knuckle down again.

He packed up what was left of the supplies, but noticed the sun sinking over the hills to the west right about the time he finally decided to march up to Willow's door this evening and lay everything on the line.

AFTER CHANGING INTO her painting clothes, Willow finished a good share of the exterior front wall by noon. She half expected Coop to quit the job he was doing, drive down and get ready to leave. But he didn't. If she stepped over to the edge of the house he was visible much of the time. He looked fine. Too fine for her peace of mind.

Upset by that, she cleaned up her paint mess by about five and began to fix supper. It was late enough that she assumed Coop would want to eat before he took off. Exhausted, Willow didn't think she had the energy to face Coop again. Closing her eyes, she felt her resolve to send him away weaken.

For that reason, she went to the front window every few minutes as supper cooked, watching for him. She knew he'd clean up before walking to the house. She decided she'd just set out a plate for him.

It grew later and later. Clouds had rolled in to darken the sky, and twilight bathed everything in a shadowy pinkish gray. If not for the fact that Coop's pickup and horse trailer hadn't moved, Willow might wonder if he'd taken her at her word and simply left.

At the thought of that, an ache settled in her heart. *What did you expect?* She'd issued that edict for the... what—fifth time? Sixth? And yet she felt so ambivalent. Was she that pathetic?

She fed Lily early. Willow's stomach was too jumpy; she couldn't eat any of the meat loaf she'd made for Cooper. She'd chosen his favorite meal she realized, as she prepared his plate and covered it with foil. Between dashing to the window to peer out, she washed pots and pans to steady her nerves. The sporadic rumbling of thunder added to her anxiety as she waited. And waited. Waited for any sign that Coop was coming to eat his last meal at the ranch. Or...he'd been eating inside this past week. What if he expected to do that tonight? It would be difficult. But his going away was inevitable. It had to be.

Despite the heaviness of her heart, Willow argued with an internal voice that continued to ask why she was sending him away. "Because it's right," she answered out loud. "This is a no-win situation."

Lily glanced up from her plate, her hazel eyes curious, or so it seemed to Willow. She was fascinated by Coop, reveled in his attention. And so did Willow. But therein lay the whole sad truth of it. At the moment they were like a new project to Coop. Eventually he'd tire of them. Coop Drummond was like a rolling stone. He'd abandoned her for the rodeo. Now he'd left the rodeo, but he wouldn't commit to working on the Triple D. Whatever was next on his agenda, Willow couldn't allow her daughter's fragile heart to be caught in the wreckage Cooper Drummond was sure to leave behind.

Chapter Nine

In another hour the sky had gone black to the south. The air was heavy and smelled like impending rain. Willow went out to store her paint supplies in the shed, where they'd be safe from high winds. If a bad storm blew in, the trim would have to wait. Summer storms generally passed through quickly.

Shading her eyes, she scanned the hills for some glimpse of Cooper. She heard the bawling of steers, so she assumed he was rushing to finish. Assuming he'd be late, she turned down the oven heat to keep the plates warm. She hoped he'd show up to eat soon and then leave—just to end her anxiety.

She bathed Lily and dressed her for bed. The little girl trekked back and forth to the screen door a dozen or more times in her pajamas. It was plain to Willow that her daughter was missing Coop. She'd gotten used to coloring with him and listening to him play his guitar every evening. Both of these things spelled progress for a child who had been so withdrawn. Coop had called it a breakthrough, and maybe it truly was. Anything that brought Lily out of her world, even for a brief period, was a good sign. Coop had helped Lily overcome previous deficiencies in fine motor skills and coordination. She did less toe walking now; not walking with the whole of her foot was another symptom of autism. Some kids flapped their hands or banged their heads. Lily had done all of them. Before these evenings with Cooper, though, nothing except a loud noise could stop Lily from rocking with her rabbit. Lately, she'd been scooting close to hear Cooper's music as if she derived pleasure from it, and that was noteworthy.

All the same, Willow couldn't help worrying. Her main fear was that when Coop left—and it'd always been a matter of *when*, not *if*—Lily would backslide. The visiting nurse and the book on autism both stressed the value of consistency in an autistic child's environment. It stood to reason that it would be better for her if he left now, before she grew too dependent on him.

It had grown late, and Willow insisted that Lily, who was clearly tired because she rubbed her eyes so often, stop waiting by the door for Coop. Lily fussed, unwilling to go to bed.

Willow brought the radio into her room. They couldn't get many stations at night, but she spun the dial until she picked up a Tejano station from across the border, one with mariachi music and little talking. It seemed to satisfy Lily enough to allow Willow to read two children's books. Worn books she'd bought long ago at the grocery store, although Tate thought books were frivolous, unimportant. Willow forced her mind off Tate. It did no good to remember. In fact, it made her wonder if, as Coop had intimated, she'd been cowardly not to leave Tate when Lily was first diagnosed. And it was true that by then Tate had destroyed any feelings she'd ever held for him. She'd made so many mistakes when it came to Tate. Her biggest had been to marry him, thinking she'd grow to love him. She'd done them both a disservice. But when they were kids, Tate had been fun. He used to slip funny cards and small gifts into her book bag. During high school he walked her home when Coop wasn't around. In college she was involved with Coop, but Tate was always around in the background. After Coop went off to rodeo, Tate had consoled her, and he was particularly kind to her and her mother at the time of her dad's death. She'd mistaken his attention for love, she realized with a sigh, bending to kiss Lily's forehead before starting another story.

Midway through *The Tale of Peter Rabbit,* Lily fell asleep. Willow set the book aside, turned down the radio and shut off the light. A princess night-light her mother had sent for Lilybelle's first birthday glowed rosily along the baseboard. It was a shame her mother came up with one excuse or another not to visit. Although it took a while, Willow eventually figured out that her mother preferred to be a grandmother from afar. Willow walked out of Lily's room, leaving the door ajar.

Should she put Coop's plate on the porch, store the remaining meat loaf and go to bed? Willow couldn't resist going to the window for one last check to see if Coop had gone while she was reading to Lily. The Dodge Ram hadn't moved, nor had he attached the horse trailer yet. Relief ricocheted through her, even though it probably just meant that he was too tired to hit the road tonight. With luck she'd catch a final glimpse of him in the morning, although watching him drive off would hurt.

As she removed his still-warm plate from the oven, she heard heavy boot treads on the front porch. Willow froze. Her stomach churned, then her heart leaped at his sharp rap on the front door.

Unsure what to do, she set the plate on the counter. The knocking grew insistent, forcing her to hurry. The old living-room wall clock ticked loudly, although her heartbeat seemed, to her own ears, even louder. "I'm coming," she called, keeping her voice down. "Stop pounding, or you'll wake Lily," she admonished as she flipped on the porch light and opened the door.

She held her breath as Coop braced a hand on the casing. He must have bathed in the pond, she decided, since his hair was damp and spiky. He wore different clothes than he'd had on when she confronted him earlier. A whiff of soap wafted through the screen, tickling Willow's nose. The picture he presented including his crooked smile, evoked an image of Coop naked in her pond. Her stomach tensed as Willow harked back to happier days when they could hardly keep their hands off each other. Days when Coop knew and loved every inch of her body. Steeling herself against those memories and the longings they brought, Willow gripped the door tightly, reminding herself that she couldn't afford to think only about *her* needs and desires.

"It's late, Cooper. Lily's in bed asleep," she said in a hushed voice. "If you've come to say goodbye, there's no need. I thought we handled that earlier. If you want a meal, I'll bring it out."

Coop jerked open the screen and stuck the toe of his

boot firmly in the crack to prevent Willow from slamming the door in his face. "I had all afternoon to think about your carefully prepared orders giving me my walking papers, Willow. There was a time I was sure we'd always be together, you and I. All those days and nights we talked about our future, it never crossed my mind that I'd ever lose you."

"Coop." Willow sagged against the door, pressing it hard against his foot. "We both made choices that took us in different directions. What's done is done. We can't go back."

"Are you telling me you never think about the plans we made together?"

She swallowed the lump in her throat. "Those plans never included you running off to rodeo. The first time you said a word to me about it was two weeks before your college graduation. That was a deal-breaker for me, Coop, and I never hid my feelings."

"I know, but my going off to rodeo had nothing to do with you—with us. I did it to piss off Sullivan as much as anything. That sounds immature…but my brother still thought he could manage my life. Going on the circuit gave me breathing room. And you were planning to attend summer school. I figured you'd have your degree and be waiting by the time I came back. I didn't intend to stay on the circuit so long."

"You never asked me to wait! You sold your horses and took off for Mesquite. Sullivan's the one who told me where you'd gone when I called you at the Triple D to let you know my dad started having seizures, and Mom asked me to drop out of college to stay with him."

"When was that? Sully never said a word about you calling me."

"Yes, well, he seemed to think I'd given you an ultimatum—marry me or go rodeo. I felt you didn't care what I thought, Coop, and you certainly never asked me to wait."

"Would you have waited if I *had* asked?"

Willow lifted her eyes and met his dark, steady gaze. Thunder rolled overhead. "Honestly? I'm not sure. I loved you, Coop, but it ripped my heart out to know you could be injured like my dad. I tried telling Sully that later, when he accused me of not loving you enough to keep you from going off. He all but called me selfish. In hindsight, maybe I was. Your leaving practically destroyed my world."

"What do you think happened to mine the day I heard you'd married Tate?"

She shook her head. "I hadn't heard from you once after you left. You didn't even call when my dad died."

"I was at the finals. But I sent flowers. By then I'd heard you were seeing Tate, and that made me crazy."

"We weren't exactly seeing each other. He turned up everywhere I went." She released the door and gestured with one hand. "What's the point of rehashing all of that now? You slept your way through a dozen rodeo groupies before I married Tate. Don't deny it—your exploits made the covers of rodeo trade magazines."

Coop clenched the hand still braced on the door. "None of the women I hooked up with for a night meant *anything* to me, Willow. I never knew why until it hit me today. I measured all those women against you. You're who I dreamed about, Willow."

"You also dreamed of becoming a rodeo champ. God, Coop, how many times did you watch me feed Dad, who was paralyzed from the neck down? I knew only too well where rodeo dreams led."

"You're wrong. I never dreamed of being a champion bronc rider. It's like I just told you. I thought you and I were solid, and I had to get away because Sully tried to take Dad's place and he wasn't Dad." He paused. "I'm sorry, but I assumed you understood that." Coop straightened and spread his hands, forcing Willow's gaze to travel the length of his long, lean body. She glanced away, but the pressure she applied to the door eased, and Coop pushed his way into the house with little resistance.

"I promise you I'm done with rodeo now. I have a suitcase filled with championship buckles, but they make cold bedmates."

"Is that what's on your mind tonight? Getting into my bed? I've grown up, Cooper. I'm no longer starry-eyed. Life's taught me some valuable lessons when it comes to priorities. You left Hondo five years ago, just walked away. I don't know what you expect now, Coop. And don't look at me like that." The intensity in his eyes made her knees go weak, but Willow raised her chin, standing her ground.

He touched her chin, running his thumb over the slight cleft. "I let you go once. I'm not inclined to walk away again. You say you want me to leave, but your eyes tell a different story. We have a lot of history, Willow. Most of it was good."

"Some of it wasn't," she said, jerking her chin away from his hypnotizing touch.

"I can't undo what I did in my youth."

"Would you change it if you could? If we could go back, Cooper, would you *not* go off to ride bucking horses?"

"I can't say that. Even if I'd stayed at the Triple D back then, my life would have revolved around raising horses, and green horses buck. If you want to know if I have regrets about how I handled myself with you and Sullivan, that answer is yes. I shouldn't have left you without doing a better job of explaining my reasons. And I regret blowing my winnings when I could've saved so I'd have some money to show for those years. But maybe things happen for a reason. If I'd had cash to, say, invest in breeding stock, I wouldn't have ended up here asking you for a second chance. Will you give me one, Willow?" He stepped closer, holding her gaze as thunder rumbled overhead and the first raindrops blew in the door.

Cooper had never lacked charisma, Willow thought. He drew her. His energy. His heat. The security he offered. Long-term security was something Willow hadn't let herself want for a long time. But while she analyzed Coop's motives, he closed the gap between them, kicked shut the door and took her in his arms.

He mumbled words that sounded like *I love you*. She couldn't be sure if he'd said it or if she'd imagined he had. Either way, the past suddenly seemed to melt away. There was only the here and now. And it wasn't so difficult to believe he'd spoken the words. Coop had always said he'd loved her; deep down she'd always loved him. She set her hands on either side of his neck where his pulse beat fast. "You never left my heart," she murmured, pressing lightly against him. "You're still there."

HER TOUCH WAS WARM and honest, but Coop didn't want to move too quickly. He wanted to be sure she was giving him the green light. This was happening fast even though the time and distance that had once separated them seemed to disappear. In the muted lamplight spilling into the living room from the kitchen it was as if Willow hadn't changed. The look of her, the feel of her soft skin under his fingertips as he stroked her neck, sent Coop reeling back in time.

His mouth covered hers. First, like a whisper, then demanding—and receiving—a response. Coop's thumbs skimmed her cheeks with restless abandon, as his hands tilted up her face.

Willow wanted him with a never-forgotten hunger. It felt right, natural, to pick up where they'd left off five years ago. In a rush of hot kisses and hastily discarded clothing, they tumbled together on her living-room carpet.

Coop hauled in a deep breath. He braced himself on hands and knees and planted wet, openmouthed kisses on her skin, moving from the pulse that beat frantically in her neck to her navel. There he traced her belly button with his tongue.

She shook so hard she fell back and let Coop take the lead. Their initial coupling, out of necessity, was hurried. As the old familiar heat enveloped Willow, she opened for him.

Coop gave, too, and Willow took. It'd been so long

since she'd felt anything toward a man but duty. And after Lily's birth, her love life ended because Tate started coming home so drunk he passed out. She sensed that Tate had used sex to punish her during the early days of their marriage; there'd been little pleasure and less love.

Now, with Cooper, Willow felt cherished. She felt equal. Powerful. Coop had been her first teacher, her first lover. She was glad she hadn't forgotten how to participate. How to be a giving partner. Kissing him, she slid her hands down his leanly muscled waist to his tight butt and back up his narrow hips. "It's not fair that your skin feels like silk." She sighed, nipping his earlobe.

Coop groaned and drove deeper.

Willow cried out and Coop reared back. "Did I hurt you?" he asked.

She shook her head wildly and urged him on until a series of spasms rocked her from head to toe.

Rolling over, Cooper flopped both arms out to his sides. "I feel like a jellyfish," he said. Edging up on his elbows, he asked again if she was okay.

"If a rag doll can be fine, I'm great. I shouldn't add to your ego, but the word *cataclysmic* comes to mind," she said, ducking her head to press tiny kisses to his chest.

He laughed and Willow felt the rumble in her ear.

"You can't be comfortable, Coop. Why don't we move to my bedroom where there's a soft bed?"

Coop ran his hands up and down her bare back, but he didn't respond to her question.

Willow lifted her head and in the faint light noticed

him frowning. "Is something wrong?" she asked, scraping back her long hair, which had come loose during their lovemaking.

"I vote for the couch," he said. "It's closer."

"And lumpy."

"Your bedroom is next to Lily's. We don't want to risk waking her."

Willow was beginning to get the feeling that Coop was protesting too much. She wriggled, trying to get off him, but he clamped his arms around her waist to hold her in place.

"The truth is, Willow, I don't want to make love to you in Tate's old bed. If you want my opinion, we did fine right here. Or I'm game for the couch."

She didn't like the fact that he was still hung up on Tate. Especially now, after the way she'd given him all she had to give, which was much more than she'd ever shared with her husband. The glow began to fade. Would Tate always come between them?

Coop stopped her retreat with kisses and caresses. His onslaught this time was more deliberate, more languid.

Willow shivered when he kissed his way up her neck and coaxed a response from her lips. She loved kissing Coop. She always had. To finally have him where she could touch him and be touched by him made her a prisoner of her own desire.

Their second round of lovemaking was slower but more thorough. When it was over, Willow rested her head on Coop's broad shoulder. "This time was more than cataclysmic," she murmured. "I feel like the whole house just shook."

Cooper traced the narrow bridge of her nose. "It did, sweetheart. That's serious thunder. The storm just broke." As he spoke, lightning flashed outside and lit the room through the uncurtained front window.

Willow sat up and reached for her shirt and shorts. "That was close. The last storm scattered my herd. They smashed down the fence in about five places. It took a week to find them all." She'd turned her back to him, but had her clothes on by the time Coop sat up and reached for his pants.

"I'm pretty sure the fence will hold this time, Willow. My guess is they'll take shelter under the trees. It's where most of them went during the branding." He was much less self-conscious about dressing in front of her. He didn't put on his boots or shirt, but smiled and took her in his arms for another kiss. "I love the energy that comes with a storm, especially the first storm to hit after a drought. Let's go sit on the porch and watch Mother Nature's handiwork, shall we?"

"I'd like that," she said shyly. "You go on out. I want to check on Lily."

"Is she likely to wake up and be scared by the thunder?" he asked as another long, loud roll rattled the windows in the house. "If so, we can stay here, or go sit by her bed." He trailed a hand down Willow's arm and linked their fingers.

That small act of thoughtfulness released a gush of warmth inside her. Any sign of caring had been missing for all of her marriage. It endeared Coop to her as nothing else could. Rising on tiptoes, Willow kissed him. "Thank you for your concern, Cooper. Lily generally sleeps like a log. But I always check on her several times a night. She sleeps. I'm the insomniac."

"Hmm." Coop helped himself to several more kisses before he drew back, patted her backside and let her go. "I can think of several ways to spend a wakeful night," he said. "Or we can work on finding new ways," he promised with a wink. "After the storm passes."

She shooed him toward the door.

As soon as she emerged from the house they cuddled together on the porch and watched the fury of the rain, thunder and lightning.

Willow felt safe cradled in Coop's arms. She told him that and added, "I didn't realize how off-kilter I've felt the past several years. I slept with one eye open, worrying about Tate's erratic moods. After his death I worried about danger from other people. I slept poorly any time I had hired cowboys on the property. I had to discourage a couple of them with one of Tate's old shotguns. It only dawned on me, Coop, how much better I've slept since you showed up."

"And yet you were ready to toss me off the ranch."

She released a heavy sigh. "Because I know you can't stay, Coop. You haven't resolved anything with your brother. And there's still the Triple D. It's partly yours."

The arm around her tightened. "Yes, but you're going to sell your herd and your ranch. Then you'll be free to go north. Any news from your Realtor, by the way? Has he received any inquiries since the day we saw someone giving the place a once-over?"

"I left him a message—I haven't heard back. But

then I've been outside painting, and maybe missed a call. I don't have an answering machine."

Coop traced her lips with one finger. "If you don't hear by the time the trim's finished and I get the herd to market, we'll drive into town and make sure he's actively working for you. Hey, this storm's petering out. What do you say we go back inside and take up on the couch where we left off on the floor?"

"Coop," she said, head bent. "You are way more open about sex than I am."

He crooked a forefinger and raised her chin so he could look into her eyes. "Know this, Willow. It's always been about more than just sex between us."

She nodded shyly.

Coop carried her back inside, where they gave the lumpy old couch a workout until they fell asleep wrapped in each other's arms.

Willow's internal clock woke her at her usual time—five o'clock. The day was dawning hot and humid again, but she stole an extra five minutes to remain snuggled up against the man she loved. The man who'd shown her in so many ways throughout the night that he loved her, too, as they whispered sweet things to each other. She didn't think Coop had said he loved her in so many words, but maybe he had....

She felt herself smiling. He looked totally relaxed in sleep. She imprinted every naked line of his lean, muscular body on her mind before she bent and tickled him, then kissed him awake. "Time to get up, sleepyhead," she whispered when his eyes opened and he grabbed her. "Lily's an early riser. We can't risk having her pop out and finding us together like this. After we get dressed I'll make you a ham, cheese and mushroom omelet."

"I'm thinking about taking your mind off food...."

She climbed over him and off the narrow couch, and dressed quickly in the clothes that lay wadded on the floor. "I'm a sensible mother and rancher, yet I can't believe how tempted I am by your suggestion, Cooper Drummond. And aren't you ashamed of yourself for leading me astray?" She gathered up his jeans and shirt and tossed them at him.

He jackknifed up, his brown eyes laughing, his dark hair rumpled. "Not on your life, sweetheart. Not on your life."

Chapter Ten

In the kitchen, after they'd each taken a turn freshening up in Willow's small bathroom, Coop made his coffee and put water on for Willow's tea while she assembled the ingredients for their omelet.

Reaching over her to take down plates, he rubbed his chin on top of her damp hair. "We're pretty good at this. Anybody might think we're an old married couple."

She ducked away and pulled out the chopping board with shaky hands. "Have you ever thought about getting married, Cooper? I mean, have you ever come close?"

He paused in the act of setting the table. "Not after you dumped me."

"Hold on. Who dumped whom?"

"Okay. After we split. I never found any woman I cared to invite to the next rodeo."

"Oh, really?" she scoffed.

"I swear. The women who competed in rodeo events were just buddies. The hard-core followers, you know, like the ones you saw in the restaurant, are superficial."

"They looked beautiful."

"Yeah, well, I'll give them points on that score. A

few may have been on the prowl for husbands. The rest were just on the prowl. Out for a good time. They flocked around winners."

"I noticed," she murmured, beating the eggs. "Of course, you were a champion most of the years you competed."

"Five years. I called it quits at the beginning of last season and started earning an honest living," he joked, tweaking the end of her ponytail. He was saved from having to defend his wild bachelor days by the sudden appearance of a sleepy-eyed Lily. She wandered into the kitchen, rubbing an eye with one fist, dragging her rabbit by an ear with the other.

"Hey, there, babycakes," Coop said, dropping down on one knee to put himself at her level.

She quit rubbing her eye and blinked solemnly at him.

"What does she eat for breakfast?" Coop asked Willow. "Most kids don't like omelets. Not the stuff in them like mushrooms and onion, anyway."

"Right on all counts. She'll eat a biscuit with jelly, no butter, and bacon. But the bacon I put in the oven to warm can't touch the edges of her biscuit."

"Why? They all mix together in your stomach."

"I don't know. That's something I've learned from observation. It's a fetish with some autistic children. Come to think of it, she's never had anyone but me prepare her meals. Why don't you watch the omelet and I'll take her into the bathroom, them I'll fix her breakfast." Willow smiled. "I'm so lucky she's potty trained."

Rising, Coop took the spatula. "Those other quirks

are symptoms I'm assuming will be addressed and modified once she starts in a proper school."

Willow glanced up from cutting the biscuit in half. "Maybe. The curriculum I read about was quite comprehensive." Frowning a bit, she grew quiet. She left with Lily, then returned after a while and lifted the child into her makeshift booster seat, removed the toy rabbit and pushed her plate closer.

"Everything's ready," Coop announced, deftly cutting the omelet in half and sliding it onto two plates already holding buttered toast. He poured himself a second cup of coffee and handed Willow her tea.

"You know your way around the kitchen, Coop. I must admit that surprises me."

"I got tired of eating out so much. If I had a block of time between rodeos, I booked into residence motels— one bedroom with a kitchen and living room. Young guys on the circuit often travel with motor homes. Those camps are a hotbed of activity and some of them party day and night. Married guys usually had a home base. Unmarried older riders get tired of the hullaballoo and they went to motels."

"Oh, yeah, you're so old." Willow laughed, cutting into her omelet. "Aren't some contenders thirty-five or forty before they quit?"

"Not too many. A few diehards. Trick riders and ropers hang in longer. Maybe the guys who really have rodeo in their blood. But it takes brute strength and agility to keep riding sixteen- or seventeen-hundred pounds of bucking horse day in and day out. Casey Tibbs, the greatest bronc rider of all time, stayed with the sport eleven years. I guess I never got so addicted to the roar of the crowds that I couldn't let go. I prefer life a little quieter."

"Last night you said you like it here, Coop," Willow ventured. "You said you might want your own ranch." Idly she spun her fork in an uneaten portion of omelet. "You even said you could stay here. Did you mean it?"

"I meant it. But you're the reason why. You might not think I'd be lonely on the rodeo circuit with so much action. But I sorta like coming in after a day of hard, satisfying work out on the range, being able to sit down with you and talk. Or say nothing, for that matter."

"What about the Triple D?"

Coop pushed back his empty plate. "What about it? You're not there. And Sully's put his stamp all over it. This is a great little place that could be a lot better. I could make it better for you and the munchkin. On the other hand, Lily needs the facilities offered in a bigger town." His gaze cut to Lilybelle, who'd licked the jelly off both halves of her biscuit and was now eating her bacon. "The sun's getting high," Coop said as he rose from his chair. "It'll be a sauna out there soon. You wanted to paint the trim. And, if it's okay with you, I thought I'd start trying to break a colt that's taken up residence on your upper forty. The colt and his mother are half-wild. There's open range down in Mexico, and I figure they strayed here. Once he's broken, the colt can be gelded and will bring you a pretty penny. Enough to tide you over until you decide whether to restock your cattle, or sell and move on."

"I'd consider restocking if you stayed, Coop. Although I'd have to find a way to get Lily the services she needs." Willow sighed. "I'd never send her to boarding school." Rising, too, she collected their plates. At the sink, she ran water and rinsed them. Her back remained rigid as she waited for Coop's response.

Stepping up behind her, he turned her around and delivered a steamy kiss. "I want to be with you," he said. "A man needs a good woman." Moving toward the table again, he pressed a softer kiss on Lily's curls. "And a family," he added.

The girl hunched her little shoulders and screwed up her face, but instead of crying as Willow feared, Lily brushed a hand over her head, stared at Coop and gave a passable giggle.

Willow clutched her heart. "That's another first. A huge one."

"See?" Coop said. "I'm good for her. Maybe we can look into schooling her ourselves. With a satellite dish we could go online for help."

"Is that true? Cooper, you're good for both of us. You give me something I've had so little of—hope that Lily's life can be better."

Coop picked up his hat. "So, uh, maybe you should call your Realtor and take the ranch off the market. However, don't let me influence you. It has to be your decision, Willow."

She gnawed the inside of her mouth. *Was that a commitment or not?* So many worries and concerns flashed through her head. There before her stood the man she'd always loved. Big and bold. Solid and sexy. With his encouragement and assistance, perhaps they could school Lily and make her life happier. "I'll phone

Marcus Realty today," she said, knowing she sounded tentative.

Coop bobbed his head and turned to leave. "Okay. Sure."

Sobering, Willow gripped the fabric of her blouse at the base of her throat and called out to Coop. "I know you read my book on autism. I know you're enthusiastic about her progress—and helped make it happen. But I have to tell you that the doctor and counselor said she'll likely never catch up with other kids her age. There's no magic potion or cure-all for autism, Cooper."

He started to say they'd do whatever they could, whatever was necessary to improve Lily's quality of life, but he was stopped by the sound of a car pulling into the driveway out front. He lifted the curtain and huffed out a jerky breath. Muttering a surprised curse, Coop dashed for the door, letting the screen slam behind him.

Slower to react, Willow crossed the kitchen to move the curtain, allowing her to peer outside. She didn't recognize the vehicle, a late-model silver SUV. It wasn't the one that had passed the ranch the other day.

Willow would have gone back to work and let Coop deal with the stranger but then he yanked open the SUV door—and out crawled a shapely woman with a lot of red hair. She wore jeans, boots and a bright yellow shirt that should have clashed with her hair, but somehow looked fashionable instead.

Willow's mouth went slack as she watched Coop, the man who'd recently left her after a night of loving, haul the redhead into an embrace that went on far too long. At least that was how it looked to Willow. A sick feeling washed over her. She let the curtain slip through trembling fingers as the old insecurities flooded her. She'd seen enough, yet couldn't resist gawking. She was well aware that Cooper Drummond collected women. The pair had parted, but Willow saw them grinning at each other. Then they walked toward Coop's pickup, his arm casually looped around the other woman's narrow waist.

Her legs gave out, and Willow dropped into the nearest kitchen chair. The one where Coop had sat to eat his breakfast. She covered her hot face and wept quietly. Once again he'd shattered her hopes and dreams. But why was she surprised? She'd witnessed for herself how he had acted with those female fans at the restaurant. She remembered how Tate used to rub it in about Coop's exploits with women along the rodeo trail. He swore the stories printed in the rodeo trade magazines were true. Of course they were. Cooper would have all the women he wanted. He was gorgeous—and available.

THE MINUTE COOP recognized the silver SUV, he'd dreaded going out. But he didn't want to create a scene in front of Willow, either. Once outside, he was relieved to have his sister-in-law, Blythe, emerge from the vehicle; he'd been so sure it was, Sully come to confront him over his request for money.

Cooper guided Blythe away from the house, into shade provided by a stand of live oak, because there was no sense involving Willow in his money woes until he learned what had brought Blythe here. As it turned out, he didn't have to ask, she volunteered.

"You're looking good, Cooper." Then she got right to the point. "I came to bring you a check." She handed him a folded blue square she extracted from her back pocket. "Sully said the other day that you'd phoned and needed money."

"Sully sent you?"

"Not exactly."

Coop glanced at the check. It was for ten thousand dollars, twice what he'd requested from his brother. "This is drawn on your clinic account, Blythe." Coop raised an eyebrow. "I can't take money from you." He tried to hand it back.

She curled her fingers around his, urging him to pocket the check. "We're all family, Coop."

"Does Sully even know you've come to see me? Does he know you're bringing me this kind of cash?" He waved the check.

"I doubt I have to tell you how stubborn he can be sometimes."

"Sometimes?" Coop flared.

"Yes, sometimes. Mostly he's a softie." Blythe's eyes were tender as she said that. "Sully has unlimited patience with Gray. And he's a wonderful husband to me. I feel a certain amount of guilt for canceling appointments today to come and see you, Coop. But darn it, I want you two to reconcile. You're *brothers*. Not only that, the Triple D is too much work for Sully alone."

"He hires ranch hands. And I heard he advertised for a part-time manager."

"Because I begged him to. It's temporary. Just until Christmas. He wants you to come home for the holidays. He's counting on it, Cooper. We're all counting on it."

Coop stared at the house and at the nearby rolling hills, but he tucked the check in his shirt pocket. "Maybe there's too much water under the bridge," he mumbled.

"The Triple D is your heritage."

"It hasn't felt like it. Not since Dad died."

"That's another thing. Matt would hate to see this rift between you guys. You were the world to him, both of you, after your mom died."

"Losing Mom and then Dad tore my world apart, Blythe. Sully handled the loss much better."

"I don't think he did. He hides his pain. He keeps his anxiety bottled up inside."

Coop snorted.

"It's true." Blythe curved her right hand around Coop's tense wrist. "All I ask in return for giving you that money is that you make your way back to Hondo for a family holiday. You can stay at the home place. I'll make sure it's ready. Oh—maybe you didn't know that Sully and I built a new home closer to my clinic. So the old home is empty, waiting for you."

"I'd heard about the new house via the grapevine. Jud Rayburn told me. I'm not sure I can make you that promise. If it turns out I can't, I'll pay you back the money. Or else Sully can, because at some point he'll have to cash out my share of the ranch."

"You can bring Willow," Blythe said.

Coop swiveled his head toward her. "So you know this is her ranch?"

Blythe nodded. "Sully and I rarely keep secrets

from each other. Sometimes it takes finding the right moment to unburden, but eventually we do. For instance, I'll tell him about this trip and about the money, probably tonight. So leave Sully to me. Don't let my advancing you some funds stop you from coming home."

"Willow has a daughter," Coop said. "She's Tate Walker's kid, but Willow named her Lilybelle for my mother and hers. Lily is younger than Gray by a few years." Coop swallowed and finally murmured, "She has special needs."

"Oh, I'm sorry, Coop. If you don't mind my asking, what's the nature of her...disability?"

"She's autistic. Willow has a book on the disorder, which I read along with a couple of magazine articles. The thing is, Blythe, other than one set of tests and a meeting with some visiting professionals, she doesn't have access to help. I'm not sure if anything is even available in Carrizo Springs or the surrounding towns. Before I got here, Willow was struggling to take care of herself, her daughter and the ranch." He pulled at his bottom lip. "This place is a far cry from the Triple D, but it has potential. Willow keeps saying she wants to sell and move to a bigger city, but any time I ask if she's talked to her Realtor, she acts as if she'd rather stay here. I think she's afraid to let go of the security. So... this morning, I offered to hang around for a while."

"But I can tell you're not convinced it's the best option, Coop. You know it'd be a short drive to San Antonio from the Triple D. There are all kinds of medical services there. I can check on some if you'd like me to."

He shifted from foot to foot and stroked his jaw without comment.

"I guarantee no mother could resist an offer of top-notch care for her child," Blythe continued. "I understand Willow may not be comfortable in a big city on her own. But…she wouldn't be alone. You love her, Coop. Does she love you, too?"

Momentary guilt flickered in Cooper's eyes as they settled on his sister-in-law. "You cut right to the chase, don't you? I think the answer to both questions is yes. We're making progress. You have to understand there's a lot of baggage piled up between us."

"Big guy like you should be able to wade through any amount of baggage. It's July now. My dad is coming for Thanksgiving. Can I plan on having you, Willow and Lilybelle at the dinner table, too?"

"I thought you said Christmas. Has anyone ever told you that you can be awfully pushy?"

She laughed. "All the time. I have to be in order to make it in the male-dominated world of veterinary medicine, at least in Texas. Plus I have to show those sick horses and bulls—not to mention Sulllivan—who's boss." She raised an arm and flexed her muscles, eliciting a grin from Cooper. "Speaking of sick animals, I need to get back, but I'll spare an extra few minutes if you'd like to me talk to Willow. You know, pave your way?"

"No, but thanks. This is something I need to take care of myself. I'll walk you back to your car. And thank you for the money. Willow's herd is ready for market, but she doesn't have the cash to rent trucks. I'd about drained my account catching up on stuff that needed fixing around here. I always figured Tate was a no-good bastard, and seeing the mess he left his wife and daughter in proved me right."

"This is a pretty enough spot," Blythe said, scanning the area as they walked back to her SUV. "But it's not for you. Your legacy is up north. The Triple D has grown a lot since you left. I'm probably being selfish, but for Sullivan's sake, I want you to come home. And I can see the advantages of Gray having a playmate on the property. He's a good kid, Coop. Far more sensitive than Sully will admit. I could see our son growing up to be a doctor, lawyer or accountant—maybe a vet— but not a rancher." She cleared her throat. "Uh, about Sully approaching you with the papers to make Gray a full third partner…it's nonsense. Gray is afraid of any animal larger than a kitten."

"Ouch. I bet that's tough for my macho brother."

"No as bad as you'd think," she said, hugging Coop before she climbed into the SUV. "Remember, Sully's a marshmallow inside. He loves Gray with every bit of that squishy heart. And he loves you." She pushed the starter and the engine revved.

Coop looked thoughtful as he slapped the flat of his hand on her vehicle. "I have a colt to break before we melt in the heat today, but I promise you, Blythe, I'll talk to Willow soon. The decision will be up to her," he said, tugging at his ear. "One thing I *am* sure of, I'm not going to leave her. And if we come to the Triple D, I won't stand to have Sully causing her pain or distress. She told me he wasn't nice to her the last time they met. He blamed her for not stopping me from going off. As if she had some power over me that he lacked."

"Family dynamics are complicated. Sully says stuff

without thinking sometimes. But he needs you. He's become a workaholic."

"Doesn't he know that's what killed our dad at such a young age?" Coop asked.

"Bless you for realizing that." Sliding out of the seat, Blythe rose on her toes and hugged Coop again. "If I'm pushing you to come home, it's because I want my husband around long enough to grow old with me. I want us both there to play with our grandchildren."

Coop slowly reached up and loosened Blythe's arms. He carried her hands to his lips and pressed a kiss to her knuckles. "Have you made Sully get a checkup? His heart's okay, isn't it?" Coop stared sharply at Blythe.

"It's not your fault, Coop, so don't blame yourself, but Sully saw the doctor in Hondo shortly after the last argument you two had. His blood pressure was sky-high. Doc Metzger put him on blood-pressure pills. Sully seems calmer now. And I've talked him into hiring a part-time manager. He's not family, though. I don't know if you're aware that your dad put a lot of pressure on Sully to look after the Triple D—and you."

Coop's chest felt tight. "High blood pressure is what caused Dad's heart attack. Tell Sully he'd better watch it." Coop let Blythe slide into the driver's seat, then jammed his hands in his back pockets to keep them still as she urged him once more to come home for the holidays. He watched her until she drove out of sight.

She had a point. Coop needed to go home, even if it was only a short visit to square things with Sully. Maybe Blythe didn't intend to hurt him with her message, but it left him feeling raw. He should've gone inside to discuss everything with Willow right away.

but he had a lot to mull over first. She didn't have any warm feelings toward his brother. What would he do if she refused to go with him to the Triple D?

It would be best to sweat out the tug-of-war that seemed to be splitting his skull in two. If he went back to the Triple D for good, he'd want to work with horses again and let Sully handle the cattle. At least the Triple D was big enough to hold the six of them. Earlier Willow had expressed a preference for staying here; perhaps he should've allowed Blythe to get the ball rolling with her. A little voice in his head called him a coward—the last thing he wanted to be in Willow's eyes.

Chapter Eleven

Willow wanted to start painting the trim on the house, but she didn't want to go outside while Cooper was entertaining his latest groupie. She certainly didn't want to appear nosy. But she was hurt and curious, so she peeked around the curtains more than once. It was like rotten icing on the cake that she chose to look out just as the red-haired woman was saying goodbye. Bad enough that Coop had greeted her enthusiastically with a big hug, but as the redhead prepared to leave, she climbed into her car—only to jump back out and wrap Coop in an embrace that seemed to go on forever. And then he *kissed* her hand. No matter how many times Willow told herself not to be upset, she was. The SUV backed out and took off down the road, but Coop watched it go. Was that a new spring in his step as he finally turned to walk away? How dumb had she been to let him in her house last night? Or worse, welcome him into her bed.

Well, technically not her bed. He'd made an issue of not using the bed where she'd slept with her husband. That should have told her something. But after their incredible night, didn't Coop owe her—what? Respect? Darn right he did. Tate never respected her and she needed that from Cooper. She also needed to respect herself. The next time Coop Drummond waltzed up to her door, he'd find it shut tight—same as her heart.

Not wanting him to catch her at the window where he could accuse her of spying, she hurried to the back of the house. She made Lily's bed and straightened her room. As she passed her own bedroom, the sight of her bed, which hadn't been slept in, was a stark reminder of the hours she'd spent in Coop's arms. Small aches were magnified, reminding her of the way she'd rolled around on the living-room floor with him for half the night. They'd spent the other half together on a too-narrow sofa.

But what did their night of fantastic sex mean to Cooper? Apparently not as much as it meant to her, she thought, straining to hear him come back inside. Surely he'd pop in to pick up something to take for lunch. Despite insisting that she didn't want to see him again, she kept listening for him. She told herself to act blasé. Let him bring up his visitor. Let *him* explain all those hugs.

Minutes ticked by. There was nothing left for Willow to straighten in the house, and still Cooper hadn't come back.

Although she refused to give in to more tears, they weren't far from the surface. At last, deciding to see what was going on, Willow looped her hair up under the baseball cap she wore for painting and stepped onto the porch.

Standing at the railing, she saw Coop ride out on the sorrel gelding named Rusty. He didn't glance back. He seemed relaxed in the saddle, like he didn't have a care in the world. No, the cares were all hers, she thought bitterly.

What really broke her heart was to watch Lilybelle get up from where she sat in her usual spot on the porch, stretching out an arm toward the disappearing rider. Not one to show much—if any—emotion, Lily wiggled her fingers the way she'd taken to doing when she wanted Coop to pick her up. Her expression as she turned to her mother was one of bewilderment. He'd made so much progress with Lily. And now, after canoodling with his morning visitor, it was plain he didn't give a damn about that or anything else.

How could she have been so gullible? "I think it's a good thing I didn't call the realty office and cancel the sell order on our ranch, honeybee." Willow walked over to where Lily had again plopped down with her rabbit.

Kneeling, Willow touched her child's shoulder. "Say, Bye-bye, Coop.' We won't see him again until suppertime. If then." Rising, Willow couldn't admit how suddenly she felt a pang at the thought that perhaps they wouldn't ever see him. She tried to shake off her concern; after all, it was only yesterday she'd tried to send him away. She hadn't convinced him to go, but maybe his visitor had.

Willow brought Lily a handful of animal crackers and then hauled the paint supplies out of the shed where she'd stored them prior to the storm. She couldn't seem to shake her feeling of unease.

There was probably still some electricity in the air from last night's fast-moving disturbance. She couldn't blame Coop for everything. Her jumpiness might be nothing more than anxiety over climbing to the top rung of the ladder to paint the fascia at the ends of the house.

She started at the highest point, where it would be possible to see Coop in the upper pasture. How pathetic was that, she thought, grimacing as she opened the can of steel-blue paint. She spotted the sorrel's broomstick tail where the horse had been staked out in a patch of grass, but Coop was nowhere to be seen.

The blue trim looked great against the gray siding. Coop sure pegged the color right. Once finished, it'd definitely make the house more attractive.

Willow's stomach dipped again. So, did she want to sell? All the absurd planning she and Cooper had done over breakfast, when she'd coaxed him to stay here with her and Lily, boiled down to nothing of substance. It was better to move on. But was it better for Lilybelle, who'd responded to Coop? Hadn't Willow warned him not to set himself up in that role? He could play fast and loose with *her* heart and she'd recover because she'd been hurt worse. But Lily was vulnerable. She didn't deserve Cooper's careless behavior.

Willow took angry swipes at the board in both directions as far as she could reach. Then she climbed down and moved the ladder, repeating the process around the back and the opposite side of the house, all the while keeping a close eye on Lily.

She stopped for lunch, fixing meat loaf sandwiches for the two of them. Out of habit, she made extra for Coop. He didn't show up to eat it, so she bagged his and put it in the fridge.

Willow silently hoped he got a bellyache from skipping his midday meal.

Around three o'clock she finished painting, stamped the lid back on the paint can and returned her supplies to the shed. She was washing paint off her arms with the hose when a vehicle pulled into her driveway. Willow turned off the water and checked on her daughter's whereabouts. When she glanced back at the driveway, she was surprised to see the same maroon SUV that had twice driven past the house the day she and Coop argued by the fence. She hastily dried her hands on her shirttail, then fetched Lily, who'd begun rocking nervously.

Willow was further surprised to see a second vehicle pull in and park behind the SUV. A county sheriff's vehicle. Taking Lily's hand in her now-sweating one, Willow descended the porch steps. Nerves fluttered in her belly.

Had the driver of the SUV been speeding and randomly chosen her driveway to pull off the road? If so, he'd pulled in pretty far.

The door of the SUV popped open and out came Willow's former father-in-law. Stifling a gasp, Willow held Lily back.

Bart Walker was big and gruff, and smelled heavily of cigar smoke. The one time he'd visited at the start of her marriage, he'd acted as if she didn't exist. And he'd barely tolerated her presence at Tate's funeral.

Lily picked up on her mother's unrest and wrapped one arm around Willow's leg, where she clung. Feeling defensive, Willow swung her daughter up to straddle her hip.

Her brain foggy, Willow didn't fully comprehend what was happening when the sheriff approached, introduced himself as Sheriff Richards, and forced a paper into her free hand, saying, "Mrs. Walker, your deceased husband's father has filed eviction papers on this property. I need you to go inside and pack up your belongings. Do you have friends in Carrizo Springs to bunk with until you make other arrangements?"

The gray-haired sheriff had doffed his hat. He stood in front of Willow, turning it around and around in his weathered hands.

Unable to fully digest his words, Willow merely blinked at him until Bart Walker slammed his car door. Chewing on a stubby cigar, he stomped over to her. He stared at Coop's pickup and horse trailer before demanding in a gravelly voice, "Where'd you get the fancy rig? You didn't have anything like that when I came to bury my son."

That shook Willow out of her stupor. She feared this man and she wasn't about to let him know a former neighbor of his, someone who had always been at odds with his son, was on the ranch. "The rig belongs to my current hired hand. He's out on the property. What does this mean, Bart?" She shook the paper.

Walker moved the cigar to the other side of his mouth. "I heard at the feed store that you're vaccinating and branding. Maybe I'll have your hired hand do some chores for me. Good thing the iron you ordered was the Bar W. The cattle and all of this belongs to me." He waved an encompassing arm.

Despite the hot sun beating down, Willow shivered. Dredging up her nerve, she said, "Those are my cattle. Tate sold most of the stock you bought the year we got married. I developed a small herd over the past few years."

"The hell you say. I happen to know you sold ranch property to buy calves." He stabbed a finger toward the upper range. "I figure we're square, though, because you paid my loan interest over the past year."

Willow felt her world slipping out from under her feet, and all she could do was clutch Lily tighter. Why hadn't the bank mortgage officer notified her. He probably assumed she and Bart had an arrangement since she was his daughter-in-law.

Sheriff Richards stepped between her and Bart. "He has papers to show he cosigned loans on the property," the sheriff said gently. "Mr. Walker came to town last week. He paid off the bank, so everything belongs to him now except your personal belongings."

"That's nothing," Willow mumbled. "I came here with one suitcase full of jeans and T-shirts. But...Lily-belle was born here," she said. "As Tate's daughter, isn't she entitled to something? Sheriff, we hardly ever go to town. This is our home." Willow hated to beg anything of Tate's dad, but she would for her child.

"So, are you saying you have nowhere else to go?" the sheriff asked sympathetically.

Willow didn't answer. She did have that small stash of money hidden away, but she hadn't counted it in a long time, and she had no idea if there was enough for a hotel room or bus tickets.

"Mr. Walker, surely you can afford to grub stake the missus and her daughter. We *are* talking about your grandchild," the older man said pointedly.

Bart spit out the stubby cigar and ground it into the

earth with his shiny boot heel. Extracting another from a silver case he carried in his shirt pocket, he rolled it around his tongue, then lit it, snuffing the match between his thumb and forefinger. "I might be able to spare a hundred bucks," he said, puffing away. "But I'm gonna tell you, Sheriff. Tate wasn't positive the kid was his. He told me this little slut slept around."

Willow's mouth flew open. "What? That's a lie!"

The sheriff stopped her from further objections. "I need to get back to the office. I'd appreciate it if you went in and gathered your things quickly, Mrs. Walker. You two can sort this out later in a court of law."

"Fine," she said grimly. "On second thought, I don't want so much as a dime from him." She marched inside with as much dignity as she could muster considering her knees felt like water.

Fury carried her through packing two battered suitcases she pulled from the closet in Lily's room. Alternating between praying Coop would stay away until she left, and wishing he'd ride in and wipe the smirk off Bart Walker's face, Willow folded clothing into each case. She also packed the book on autism, which Coop had returned, Lily's baby album, the coloring books and crayons Coop had bought and a few storybooks Lily loved. Regretfully, there wasn't room for the colored blocks, so she left them along with the radio Coop had given her. That hurt, too. She gave it a lingering touch, then left the room.

Setting the suitcases in the hall, Willow ducked into the bathroom and counted out the cash in her tampon box. Just under two hundred dollars. Her heart sank as she stuffed the bills into her pocket, then put the box in her overstuffed suitcase. She probably shouldn't have gotten up on her high horse and refused the money Bart might have forked over. But who knew what kind of strings would be attached? If he ever grew a heart and reconsidered the loss of his only grandchild, she'd just as soon not give him any reason to sue for access.

Willow knew that the sheriff, who seemed to dislike being Bart's messenger boy, was anxious to leave, but she decided he could wait a few more minutes. Zipping into the kitchen, she cut some apples and cheddar cheese and bagged them for snacks. She took the sandwich she'd made for Cooper, and added graham crackers and string cheese for Lily—a light supper on the bus. Now, away from the man who'd uprooted her life, Willow was able to think more clearly. Unless the Greyhound buses passing through Carrizo Springs had changed from the route she'd memorized during Tate's worst binges, they had just enough time to catch the bus headed for San Antonio.

Willow considered scribbling a note to Coop, but figured Bart would destroy any note she left. She didn't doubt that he'd do everything in his power to cause Coop trouble. There were so many problems with leaving this way; at the same time, there was no reason she should fight to stay, she thought, recalling Coop's morning rendezvous with the redhead.

Sheriff Richards was waiting patiently on the porch. He relieved Willow of the suitcases. "If I were you, I'd hang on to that eviction notice." He covered a cough. "In case down the line you decide to make a case for part of the property for your daughter," he added quietly.

Willow dabbed her eyes. Determined not to shed any tears, she mumbled, "Thank you," and checked that the folded papers were still in her back pocket. But what chance would she ever have of launching a lawsuit against a powerful man like Bart Walker, who could afford a bevy of expensive lawyers?

The sheriff stowed her bags in the front passenger seat and assisted her and Lily into the back. "Sorry about the cage," he said. "But county rules say anybody I transport has to sit in back," he said.

She buckled in, then slumped down as far as possible in the seat. "It does make me feel as if I'm a criminal being hauled off to jail," she said.

The sheriff's eyes were on his rearview mirror. "Uh, hold on a minute," he said. "Mr. Walker is flagging us down. Maybe he's had a change of heart."

Bart hiked down the hill toward the car. Huffing from exertion, he leaned into the sheriff's rolled-down window and addressed Willow. "That rig—the Dodge Ram and matching horse trailer—they look too pricey for a hired hand. Do you swear it's not an outfit Tate bought? He told me he cleaned up at the gaming tables, but after checking out the barn and shed, and figuring how much dough I sent over the years, I'm coming up short. Way short."

"It's not Tate's rig. The unvarnished truth is, your son lost his shirt gambling. This ranch wouldn't be yours to repossess and the three of us wouldn't have had food on the table if I hadn't beat Tate to the mailbox every time your checks arrived. Tate was usually so drunk that I forged his signature, deposited the checks and paid our bills before he could blow the rest."

"You're pretty cheeky sittin' there behind big John Law. Strikes me you could've left him anytime. Isn't that what women do?" The man's jowly face turned red. "So don't speak ill of my son."

Willow sank back. "Sheriff, is there any reason— any legal reason—I need to stay and hear more of this?"

"No. Walker, you have your ranch. Please step away from the car. I'm doing my duty and escorting them off your land." Gunning the engine of his aging Crown Vic, Sheriff Richards gave Bart Walker a moment to withdraw his hand, then drove off.

"I owe you," Willow said tiredly. "I'm sorry to leave my hired hand to face him later today. They know each other from up north. Near Hondo," she said. "In fact, the Bar W that Bart owns would make ten of this place. I find it odd that he's waited until now to come and claim it."

The sheriff drummed his fingers on the steering wheel. "I'm a public servant and owe everybody in my jurisdiction equal treatment under the law. All I can say is, maybe for the sake of your sweet girl, it'd behoove you to try and file a claim."

"Lilybelle *is* Tate Walker's child," she stressed. "It's never crossed my mind that I might need to prove it."

"I don't doubt she is," the sheriff said, connecting with her eyes in the rearview mirror.

"I appreciate that. Do you know if the San Antonio bus still stops at the Carrizo Springs depot at six-twenty? If I can afford tickets, it's the bus I'd like to catch."

"We'll make it with ten minutes to spare. I rarely

carry much cash when I'm working. If twenty bucks will make the difference to you getting tickets, I'll toss it in your kitty."

"You are a nice man. Unless the price has gone up a lot since last I checked, I have enough." She likely had plenty to buy the tickets, but she was worried about what she'd do when they got to San Antonio. She'd have to work that out later. If she was careful, she probably had enough for a night at a motel. Failing that, there were Salvation Army shelters.

Willow felt guilty knowing she still owed Coop a lot. Despite how things had apparently disintegrated after breakfast, she hated to leave him to confront Bart Walker without warning. But Coop was a grown man. He could stand up to Bart.

Staring out at the passing scenery, she wondered how Coop would handle the situation, knowing he'd forked out his own money on her ranch—for paint, for feed, for vaccines and food—only to have a man he disliked almost as much as Tate come and claim it all.

Memories of Coop's touch, of the night they'd shared, filled her with a rush of emotion. Foolish or not, some part of her would always love Cooper Drummond.

"There's the bus you want to catch just pulling up in front of the depot. It's early by fifteen minutes. I'll park here to let you and your girl out to buy fares. I'll fetch your bags."

"Oh, boy. People will really think I'm being run out of town." Willow made a face, but nevertheless she slid out after the sheriff opened the door for her and Lily.

"Why care what anyone thinks?" Richards asked.

"You and I know the truth. When you get to your destination, you'll likely never see any of your busmates again."

"True. Some people in this town have gossiped about me, though. You know what? I can't even complain about that. Their rumors brought someone out of my past to that ranch, and my real regret for leaving like this is knowing I've left him to deal with—well, I had no choice, did I?"

"Huh?" The sheriff removed his hat and scratched his head as his passenger swept up her child and rushed off to the ticket counter. She was still counting out crumpled bills when Richards deposited her bags at her feet. He didn't tip his hat and wish her good luck until he saw that she had enough money to cover the price of two tickets with some left over.

"Thanks for the lift," she told him as the bus driver stowed her bags in a compartment under the bus.

"Anytime," Richards said, smiling at her and Lily before turning to drive off. But it wasn't until they were settled in their seats on the Greyhound that Willow realized should've told him that if Cooper came looking for her, he should feel free to tell him where they'd gone.

She then decided that was longer than a long shot. The redhead must live nearby, and in the few short glimpses Willow had of her, she could see that the well-put-together woman didn't spell half the trouble for Coop that she and Lily did. He might even be relieved to be rid of her and her problems. For all she knew, he'd been lingering in the field, trying to figure out how to back out of their deal.

The passengers who'd gotten off for a short break climbed back on board. The bus lurched forward, leaving behind a sinking sun that streaked the small dusty town in shades of red and orange.

Chapter Twelve

Cooper wound down a tough, hot but satisfying day of working with the colt. It was difficult to determine his precise age, but from his teeth, Coop thought perhaps he was closer to two than three. The mare, obviously his mother because they shared similar markings, had probably started life in a wild herd, been captured at some point and tamed, but she had broken free before an owner could put a brand on her. Like he'd told Willow, the horses might have drifted in from across the border. That the pair had migrated to Willow's land represented pure profit for her. Maybe he'd ask her to exclude them from a sale and keep them to begin a new herd at the Triple D—supposing he could convince her to go there with him.

The mare had bruised a hoof, causing her some lameness. The colt watched Coop warily as he tended the mare's injury. She let him get close, pick up her hoof and remove a large stone embedded beneath her swollen frog. The sharp rock had been painful. The horse acted almost grateful after Coop removed it. He fed her an apple he'd snagged from an old tree that grew on neighboring land. After she ate, the mare let Coop rub her neck and muzzle. "You're a good gal," he crooned. He had a way with horses, but it was clear that the mare had previous contact with humans.

Her colt liked apples, too, and came for his share. The pair had no doubt eaten all the low-hanging fruit. Coop's ability to climb the tree proved the biggest boon in paving the way to breaking the younger horse.

Over the course of the day Coop made up his mind to do his best to overcome any argument Willow could present for not going home with him. He'd speed up the process of gentling the mare and colt to saddle. Three days. That didn't mean he'd buck out their spirit, but it meant longer hours under the hot sun while he invested time in making friends, getting the younger horse used to human smells and used to the feel of a soft rope. The saddle could come later. They could rent a double horse trailer to pull behind Willow's pickup.

By the time the sun slipped low in the west, Coop was fried to a crisp, but he was satisfied with his progress. It felt damn fine to be doing what he loved best—working with horses. They had a lot more natural intelligence than cattle. A man could spend the same long backbreaking hours raising steers only to have them turned into steak or hamburger. Not that he was averse to red meat. But if he busted his butt breeding and raising beautiful beasts like horses, that ensured a new owner could look forward to years of pleasure.

He broke open feed sacks he'd hauled up here over the weekend and filled the cattle troughs. Coop eyed the herd as they crowded close to feed. He checked for any potential problems from either the vaccinations or from the branding he'd done. The cattle looked great. Within a week Willow could arrange for trucks to take them to the feedlot he'd negotiated with—who'd agreed to buy the whole herd. With no more cows to worry about, Willow could leave with him and let the house and property remain in the hands of a Realtor. Coop remembered her saying that she planned to cancel the sell order today. But, maybe she could list with a new Realtor—one willing to work harder for her than the current agency.

Done with the cattle, and having formulated how to lay out his proposed ideas to Willow, Coop coiled his rope and clipped it to his saddle, which he boosted onto Rusty's back. He tightened the cinch. "You old son of a gun, you've had a lazy day in the shade, chowing down on sweet grass. I'm so hungry my stomach is gnawing at my backbone. I hope Willow has supper cooked by the time I get you stabled. Phew, I smell too rank to sit down to supper with ladies. I'll need a shower first," he muttered.

Gathering the reins in one hand, he climbed upon Rusty. "'Course I could go take a dip in the pond. And I guess I could've gone back down to the apple tree to get another one." He glanced at the mare and her offspring. "Think I'll call her Ginger, because she's kind of a buckskin color."

He touched his heels to his horse, seeing no reason to linger now that he knew how to tell Willow what had happened during his sister-in-law's surprise visit. Blythe's generous check still crackled in Coop's shirt pocket. He planned to return it to his sister-in-law.

Cresting the hill that sloped down to the ranch, he stroked Rusty's neck. "I'll let Willow name the colt."

Although she might think that was silly if she'd prefer to sell the pair. There were still a lot of variables.

Even though the day was waning he could see all the way to the ranch. A blur on the road caught his eye. It was a local sheriff's car moving slowly toward town, then gathering speed. Coop followed the car's progress until it topped the hill.

He urged Rusty into a trot, not daring to go any faster for fear that the gelding might step in a gopher hole.

In spite of maintaining a steady grip on their pace, Coop couldn't ward off a shadowy premonition that sneaked in. He told himself the sheriff had only driven past the ranch. A cop car out this way didn't necessarily mean trouble. But Coop was unable to keep from remembering the day another county sheriff had tracked him down at school and broken the news that his father had dropped dead of a massive heart attack. That had been one of the worst days in his life. The appearance of a cop car could still make his guts churn.

It wasn't until he reached a spot between the house and the barn, then saw his pickup and trailer, that he relaxed a bit. Or he did until Rusty trotted around the corner and Coop faced a dark maroon SUV with heavily tinted windows. He'd seen that vehicle before. At first he couldn't place where, then it dawned on him as he swung out of the saddle. It was either the same one or a twin to the SUV he'd told Willow might be a prospective buyer for her ranch.

This could be good; it might let Willow strike a deal on the ranch, which would free her to go with him to the Triple D, leaving no loose ends. Setting aside his earlier concerns about his sweat-stained clothes, Coop looped Rusty's reins over the newly painted porch newel post and bounded up the steps to the house. He mentally crossed his fingers that the SUV owner was inside making Willow a deal she couldn't refuse.

A second later, with his hand raised to knock, Coop would be hard-pressed to say who was the most shocked, he or the man rounding the house. A man he hadn't laid eyes on in over five years and didn't care if he ever saw again.

Bart Walker. What was going on?

"You!" Walker exclaimed. "What are you doing here, Mr. Big Shot Rodeo Cham…peen?"

Coop's stomach pitched. So the SUV didn't belong to a potential buyer for the ranch. It belonged to Tate's father.

The elder Walker's sarcasm, while no surprise to Cooper, didn't bode well for Willow. But it could just be the fact that the animosity between Walkers and Drummonds had deep roots. For Willow's sake, Coop elected to play it cooler than he would have if he'd been on his own.

"Paying a social visit to your daughter-in-law, are you, Bart?" Coop drawled.

"I asked you a question, Drummond."

Coop didn't like the pugnacious set of the older man's jaw. But again he decided to be circumspect. "Willow hired me to do some chores around the ranch."

Walker guffawed. "So that's your fancy-ass color-coordinated rig over there? I knew it was too top-of-the-line to belong to some part-time drifter like she claimed."

Coop's uneasiness returned in a rush. He descended the steps, but as he cast a worried glance back at the house, he realized the lights were off and the door closed tight. "Where's Willow?"

"Gone." Bart Walker pulled out a chunky cigar, set one booted foot on the lower step, then struck a match on his heel. He applied flame to the tip of his cigar until it glowed red.

"Can you be more specific? Where did she go?" In the fast-creeping darkness, Coop met the man's glittering dark eyes through the hissing flame of the match and the choking smoke rings he puffed out. "And how?" Coop continued, waving away the smoke. "Her pickup's still parked next to the shed."

Bart snuffed out the flame, plunging them into humid darkness. "The ranch looks better than I remember. Must be your doin'. But don't expect any thanks from me, hotshot—or any payment if she still owes you."

"Why would I expect anything from you? My contract is with Willow."

"I'll just bet it is." Bart's laugh fueled a wave of anger that escalated to fury at the man's next comment. "Doesn't matter what kind of deal you had with my son's widow, boyo. I own this ranch and everything on it—lock, stock and barrel. Tate had a run of bad luck with a long drought and all. He mortgaged the place back to me. I thought his missus would make a stink over having to leave. But the sheriff was good enough to follow me out here to escort her off my property all legal like. Guess she saw fussing was pointless. Not that I owe *you* any explanation, but Willow and her kid rode into town with Sheriff Richards. Don't know what her plans are and I don't care. She was no kind of wife to Tate. Typical of a woman—she sucked my boy dry. You think he didn't tell me how high-maintenance she was? He told me all right. That and a lot more."

Cooper teetered on the edge of calling Bart a liar. He itched to wipe the smarmy sneer off the man's pudgy face. But an urgency to go and find Willow and Lily superceded his desire to flatten Bart. "I've got another horse and some personal belongings in the *barn* where I've been staying," Coop said, stressing the word. Untethering Rusty, he whirled, grinding his teeth so hard he thought his jaw might break.

"That's a surprise, you bunking in the barn! Here I figured the only reason you'd be down here instead of with your arrogant brother is for what you were gettin' on the side." The older man fell in step with Coop.

"Shut up. Just shut the hell up!" Coop opened the trailer and stripped the gelding of his saddle and bridle. Bending, he hooked the trailer to the hitch on the Ram, pulled down the ramp, then led his horse inside.

Walker spoke around his cigar. "I'll go along and check the brand on the other horse. Just to verify that you don't take more than what you own."

Incensed, Coop stalked to the barn. He haphazardly tossed clothes and shaving gear into his duffel. Slinging the bag and his guitar case over his shoulder, he backed Legend from the stall and wished his horse would kick Bart, who was indeed circling the animal to check his brand. It was all Coop could do to control his temper.

Back at his trailer, he loaded Legend, dug out his keys and unlocked the pickup door. He stowed his duffel behind the seat, tossed in his guitar, then climbed into the cab. Jabbing the key in the ignition, he glared at Bart, who stood there puffing out noxious fumes. "All I can say is I hope you rot somewhere hot for cheating your grandchild out of an inheritance that would provide her with special schooling and the other care she needs."

The pickup's headlights revealed that Bart's face had reddened in discomfort, which pleased Coop no end.

"Bah! Tate wasn't sure the kid was even his. There's no proof."

"Oh, she's Tate's daughter. A DNA test could prove it easily enough. But it's good thing you don't want to claim her," he spat. "That way you won't cause any trouble when I marry Willow and adopt Lilybelle. Because...I'll be damned proud to make that beautiful child a Drummond." Coop slammed his door, cutting off any reply the other man might have sputtered. He cranked the steering wheel hard to the left and saw Bart leap aside as the Ram's oversize tires spit gravel. It gave Coop a small measure of satisfaction.

He checked both ways at the road before pulling out. The minute his pickup and trailer were firmly on the county blacktop, Coop flushed Bart Walker from his mind. His concerns went straight to Willow. She must be sick with worry over losing the ranch, over losing a herd she'd scrimped to raise. Did she have any money? Where would she go? She'd hinted that she didn't have friends in Carrizo Springs. So why hadn't she come out to the field to find him? Had the sheriff bullied her? Or did she still not fully trust him?

Mostly Coop tried to stick to the speed limit. A time

or two the speedometer crept upward. He didn't want to shake up his horses, but he wanted to get there as quickly as possible and locate Willow. But where to look? Where might she go?

As the miles slipped past, his anger began to fade. The whole Walker clan had cheated and lied their way through life. Tate had paid the ultimate price. His much older brother, Morris, had been in and out of jail his entire life. Coop had read in the paper a few years ago that Morris was serving time in Huntsville on a burglary-assault charge. Staying mad at such a pathetic group was a waste of energy.

As his temper cooled, two things that had been on his mind prior to his run-in with Bart rose up to bother him again. Both became overwhelming when he started passing signs advertising a full-service truck stop up ahead. First, he still smelled like horse and sweat and leather. Secondly, he'd only eaten half an apple since breakfast and he'd worked hard all day under a blistering sun. Lack of food was making his head spin.

Coop didn't want to face Willow in this shape. She probably wouldn't want him to console her if he smelled like a stable. And Lily, who was extra-sensitive to odors and textures—well, why put her to a test?

Carrizo Springs wasn't so big that one woman and a child could totally disappear. What galled him was that she'd done nothing wrong. Willow and her daughter were victims. Coop reasoned the sheriff would have the resources to find her a place to stay for the night. In small towns, churches often provided for anyone down on their luck. Convincing himself that a detour through the truck stop to spruce up could only leave him in better shape to rescue Willow, Coop slowed down and pulled off at the exit. He grabbed clean clothes and shaving gear out of his duffel, booked a shower stall and ordered a double hamburger to go. It would be hot and waiting for him when he emerged.

He'd forgotten about Blythe's check until he took off his shirt. He hadn't intended to use any of his sister-in-law's money. It was too late today to bank it, anyway, but knowing he could put it in his checking account in the morning gave him some comfort. If necessary he could use it to help Willow hire a lawyer to fight Bart. Although, Willow would balk at taking charity. Coop knew that as surely as he knew his own name. He just hoped she'd be okay with him paying any bills she might have incurred through no fault of her own.

Feeling much better, he came out of the shower with a more positive outlook. He paid for his burger, then took it and his rolled-up dirty clothes back to the pickup. Coop polished off the food during the few remaining miles into town. The waitress at the truck stop had told him how to reach city hall, which housed the sheriff's office and the local jail. She verified that on a Friday there'd be a deputy on duty all night.

Coop's problem wasn't locating city hall, but finding a place to park his oversize pickup and trailer. Businesses were closed, but there were bars at both ends of the street and they were hopping. He finally found a spot a block away. The evening was warm; it would've been a pleasant stroll except that no cowboy liked to walk on concrete in boots made for riding.

His first real piece of luck came when he discovered Sheriff Richards himself at his office desk filling out paperwork. "My name is Cooper Drummond," he told the sheriff. "I'm an old friend of Willow Walker's. In fact, I've been helping out at her ranch for several weeks. I came in from her north forty after putting in a full day's work—to learn that Bart Walker's laid claim to her ranch and everything on it. He said you brought Willow and her daughter to town."

The sheriff rocked back in his chair and looked Coop up and down. "Would you be the national bronc-riding champion Cooper Drummond?" the man asked, reaching for and tearing open a packet containing a cinnamon-flavored toothpick. He stuck it between his teeth and the spicy aroma filled the air.

Coop frowned. "I am, but that has nothing to do with why I'm here. Do you know where Willow and Lily are?"

"Well, now, something she said that made no sense to me earlier makes sense now. You'd be the person out of her past she felt bad about leaving behind to deal with Walker."

"Huh?" Coop grew anxious again. All he really wanted was to track down Willow. "Leave behind? Where did she go? How?"

Snapping forward in his chair, the sheriff continued to study Coop, then gave a sad shake of his head. "I hate to tell you, son, but you're too late to hook up with Mrs. Walker and her girl. I dropped them off at the Greyhound bus stop, and they boarded the seven-twenty bound for San Antonio."

Coop slammed one fist into the palm of his other hand. "Are you sure about that? Not that I'm accusing you of lying," he added hastily. He grabbed his Stetson off the desk where he'd set it when he came in and bolted for the door. "I've got to run her down before she gets to the city or I'll never locate her."

The sheriff followed him out. "Frankly, I hope you catch her. I'm sorry I had to evict her. Her husband caused plenty of trouble in town. He couldn't hold his liquor, and he was a mean drunk. Seems to me he was cut from the same cloth as his pa. Don't know if you're aware of it, but Bart Walker spent about a week here talking to oilmen and plotting his dirty work with the bank before he called on me. In my position, being elected to serve all area taxpayers, my only avenue was to tell him I don't cotton to ill treatment of women and children. That's not the code of the West. But he left me no choice."

Coop slowed his pace. "Are you saying there's oil on Willow's ranch?"

The man took out the toothpick and put it in his pocket. "I'm saying Walker *thinks* there's oil. Somehow he heard that her neighbor to the east had drilled and brought in a gusher."

"That explains Bart's sudden interest in claiming the ranch. Jeez, I hate it when bastards like that walk off with a sweet deal."

"Maybe Mrs. Walker should bide her time. There's not a lot of honor among oilmen. Frank Krebs, the rancher who struck oil—his well went dry yesterday, I hear. It was a shallow pocket, and he's out a bundle of cash on the cost to drill. Walker might just lose his shirt."

"Couldn't happen to a nicer guy," Coop said. "Although it'll be too late to help Willow. Thanks for the information. I'll pass it along to her. Say, can you tell me if the bus she took stops anywhere along the route to San Antone?"

"Uvalde, I think. But you're too far behind to catch up. Once you find her and the girl, best you can do is talk Mrs. Walker into counterfiling against Bart Walker, asking for funds from the sale of the cattle to go into trust for the child. I mentioned it, but I'm not sure she understood that she probably has a case on behalf of her daughter."

"Thanks again. I'm pretty familiar with the back roads that crisscross Texas. Traveling to rodeos, I hit most of 'em at one time or another. I know a shortcut up from Batesville. Even pulling a trailer with two horses, I figure at night there won't be much traffic. Those buses go slower and have to stop at railroad and cattle crossings. With luck I may be able to intercept her in Uvalde."

"Good luck," the sheriff called, because Coop had already taken off at a lope. This time he paid no heed to running on sidewalks in his slant-heeled boots.

Out of town once again, he stepped on the gas. Everything went his way for ten miles. Suddenly, up ahead, Coop saw lights begin to flash at a railroad crossing. The arms came down moments before he got there.

He cursed under his breath. It was nine o'clock, and Richards said Willow's bus was supposed to leave at seven-twenty. But sometimes buses waited for stragglers, especially in these small towns.

Damn, it was a loaded cattle train. Because there was nothing he could do except wait for it to pass, he plugged his cell phone into the pickup's Bluetooth and punched in his brother's number. "Sully, it's me, Coop. Don't rag on me if you've picked up on your end. Please, just listen. Your favorite neighbor, Bart Walker, came down here and had Willow and her daughter thrown off their ranch. He claims to own it. But…we can save those particulars for another day. The upshot is, Willow took off on a bus, and I got down from the upper field too late to stop her. I'm trying to head her off, but right now I'm stuck at a railroad crossing. If I find her, I plan to convince her to come home with me to the Triple D. I intend to marry her, Sullivan."

Coop heard Sullivan cough. He raised his voice to drown out what would almost certainly be his brother's objections. "Pay attention, Sully. It's taken me far too long, but I figured out I never stopped loving Willow. If she'll marry me, I also want to adopt her daughter. Here's how it is. You hire someone to ready the home place for us and I'll work with you at the Triple D. Or you and I can hammer out a payment plan so you can buy out my share of the ranch. Hey, the train's passed. I've gotta go. You think about my offer, Sully. Talk it over with Blythe. I'll call tomorrow for your answer." Coop clicked off to silence as he ended his call. Gunning the engine, he bumped across the tracks, wanting to believe the Drummond blood that ran through their veins would move his brother to overlook old transgressions, real or perceived.

He glanced up at a yellow moon, and listened to the bleat of his phone. Obviously Sully wanted to have his say. Maybe he shouldn't have come on so strong, Coop thought, grimacing. Perhaps he should've taken more blame for their falling out. He pressed down a key to shut off his phone. First things first. Find Willow and convince her of his sincerity—and then butter up Sullivan.

Chapter Thirteen

An hour and a half into the trip Lily grew restless. Willow tried to get her to eat something, or at least drink her milk. The girl pushed both away. Willow suspected it was due to the unfamiliar surroundings. The girl didn't really cry; she made a low moaning sound as she tried to rock in her seat.

Afraid of what would happen if Lily had a full-blown meltdown, Willow's stress grew. In the new age of zero tolerance for anyone causing a disturbance in a public place, no matter what the circumstances, she worried that she and Lily might be put off the bus and left by the side of the road. Willow had heard of that happening, and she felt so tense, she couldn't even eat the sandwich she'd brought for herself.

An older lady seated across the aisle from them leaned over and gave Lily a small cardboard book she pulled from a bag at her feet. "Children hate being confined."

Willow quickly took it from her daughter's hand before she could tear any pages. "This is nice of you," she told the lady as she returned the book. "But my daughter is...she has...she's autistic," Willow finally blurted out.

"I'm sorry," the woman said with genuine feeling. "I'm going to San Antonio to care for my six-year-old grandson who has a muscular disorder. His dad's in the Air Force and is out of the country. My daughter needs to work to make ends meet, but Rory requires special help, and she's worn out. Are you on your way to visit family?"

Willow shook her head. She thought how nice it would be to count on her mother. But Belle, after too many years of being tied to an invalid husband, was finished being a rock for her daughter. "My husband died last year," Willow said, not knowing why she was sharing intimate information with a stranger except that the woman had kind eyes and was sensitive to what it was like to have a child with disabilities.

The woman smiled. "My name is Grace. Grace Templeton. You're in the same kind of fix as my daughter. And your little girl is such a pretty thing. She looks perfectly fine. My grandson wears braces on his legs," she admitted. "He can't run and play with other kids his age, and sometimes his braces rub sores on his ankles and knees."

"That must be hard for him." Willow filtered her fingers through Lilybelle's fine brown hair. Leaning down, she kissed the top of her head, feeling close to tears. Every mother hoped her kids would be happy and healthy, and she couldn't guarantee that for her child.

"I don't know much about autism," Grace said. "I have heard it's on the rise. I've seen programs on TV. Several Hollywood stars have autistic children and they're raising money for research. There's not enough research money to go around," she added, ending with a sigh.

"You're better informed than me. I don't have a TV." Willow didn't say it was because she'd sold it, along with a lot of other things to buy food after Tate died. "I'm going to San Antonio because the small towns near where I used to live don't offer the range of services or schooling Lily should have. This is our first time taking a bus."

"We're pulling into the station at Uvalde," Grace pointed out. "Late as it is, this is the dinner stop. I've made the trip several times to visit my daughter. We'll be here about an hour. There's a cafeteria-style restaurant inside. I'd be happy to either get your food, or watch her while you go through the line. This is our last chance for a meal, and we arrive in San Antonio in the wee hours of the morning. Well before breakfast."

Willow glanced out at the bright lights of a larger bus stop than that in Carrizo Springs. It would be nice to share a meal and more conversation with the kindly Grace, but Willow had to hang on to every dime. She had too little left after buying bus tickets. Not nearly enough for San Antonio. How foolish had she been to set out on her own without having made arrangements at the other end? She ought to have realized no agencies would be open when she arrived. At the time she'd just needed to flee.

"Thank you," she told her helpful neighbor. "But I brought food, so maybe we'll stay on the bus during the stop."

"They make everyone disembark here and they lock he bus, dear. I've seen people eat on benches that line the building. If you do, take care. Some odd characters hang out around bus stations."

Now Willow was more anxious. What *kind* of odd people, she wondered as she collected the bag with her lunch, and hoisted Lily into her arms. Panhandlers? Drug pushers? She wouldn't like to meet those types.

The bus driver helped her down the steps, for which she was grateful as she juggled her bag and a sleepy child. At the ranch she'd felt moderately secure. Of course she'd had Tate's old shotgun to ward off amorous cowboys. Well, not Cooper. She hadn't tried to ward him off. Thinking about him, thinking about never seeing him again, pinched her heart and made her even sadder as she sought out a bench where she sat, determined to get Lily to drink her milk. But Lily was equally determined not to....

FINALLY REACHING THE outskirts of Uvalde, Coop coaxed every bit of speed he could from the Dodge. He'd ridden in a rodeo in this town and thought he remembered where the depot was. He was relieved to be right. There were two buses parked under the canopy, and people milled about the one that was just unloading. He had to park across the street and down half a block. Bounding out, Coop locked his vehicle and hurried back to join the throng of travelers. He jostled a young couple and apologized, looking wildly around in his search for Willow.

He spotted her and Lily huddled together on a bench and his stomach relaxed. Lily clutched her rabbit. Profound relief stole Coop's breath as he darted through a crowd of people. He got trapped behind a large man and had to stretch up on his toes to keep her in sigh. He called out to Willow.

She turned her head. She thought she heard someone call her name, but decided she must be hearing things. Then Willow saw Cooper weaving in and out among passengers leaving a second bus, which had pulled in moments ago.

He jogged up to them and lifted a sleepy Lilybelle from her arms. He was flushed and breathing hard. Lily yawned, but snuggled with her rabbit against his broad chest.

Willow was so startled to see him, she was speechless.

Coop dropped down beside her on the bench, and the sentences he'd been rehearsing for miles poured out. "Damn, Willow, I was afraid I'd miss you here like I missed you in Carrizo Springs. You must've known I'd run into Bart when I rode in. Thank God the sheriff told me which bus you took. Why didn't you come to the field and get me? What if I hadn't caught up to you here? Can you get your things off the bus? We're going to the Triple D, at least for now. Listen, we'll get married as soon as it can be arranged. Then, with your permission, I'm going to adopt Lilybelle." Everything tumbled out in a rush.

Willow had difficulty piecing together his clipped sentences. Silent throughout his speech, she began shaking her head before he'd finished. "You know what, Cooper? Lilybelle and I were afterthoughts in Tate's life. We came after his penchant for booze, gambling and womanizing. Way after his need to stick it to you. This morning at the house, I saw you hugging your tall, sexy redhead. I know you can't help how women flock around you, but I'm never, ever going to play second fiddle again. Nor will I be your pawn so you can stick it to your brother."

Coop gaped at Willow, trying to understand her refusal of his less-than-stellar marriage proposal. He frowned. "What do you mean? Redhead? I don't know—wait! Are you talking about Blythe? Sully's wife, Blythe? She brought me a check." He patted his pocket. "I'd phoned and asked Sully to transfer money into my account to cover the rental of cattle trucks to move your herd to market. Sully, being Sully, lectured me, but I guess he told Blythe. She's always hated the gulf between us, so she drove down with funds from her clinic account. Blythe wants us all at the Triple D, Willow. I told her you'd have to agree, and I told her about Lilybelle. She promised to research school programs and other help for Lily B," he said, smiling at the little girl. "Oh, and on the way here, I phoned Sully and laid it on the line. I told him I'd figured out that I never stopped loving you. I said we're going to get married if you'll have me. Will you?"

In a halo of light falling from a spotlight on a corner of the depot, Willow saw the seriousness in Cooper's eyes. She knew he thought she was what he wanted. "Coop, I know you probably feel some obligation to me…after the other night. But the fact that you didn't come inside to talk after you met with your sister-in-law tells me you're not sure about this." Placing a trembling hand on his warm, solid chest, she tilted up her face and kissed him on the chin. "It's okay. Bart's showing up to claim the ranch has set you free to go back to the Triple D."

Cooper followed her mouth when Willow would have drawn back. He didn't lift his head from an intense kiss until a couple of baggy-panted teens ambled past, making catcalls.

He ignored them. "Just say yes, Willow," he urged.

Flushed and somewhat breathless, she touched one hand to his lips. "I'm not convinced you've really thought this through. You shouldn't have to argue with your brother over your choice of wife." She paused. "You left Jud Rayburn's ranch because you fought with Sully. I won't be yet another reason for you to get under his skin. It's not easy for me to sit here and say that, Coop. Yes, I married another man, but in so many ways you were always in my heart."

"We've wasted enough time, then, don't you think?" he murmured huskily, reaching out and sliding a hand through her wind-tangled hair. "What more can I do or say to prove to you that I want us to be a family?"

Lily had dropped off to sleep with her head on Cooper's shoulder. She woke with a start and blinked at him. Glancing around, she patted his shirt and mumbled something that sounded like "Blue."

Tears gathered in Willow's eyes. She clutched her throat and said in a voice tight with emotion, "Coop, your shirt *is* blue. Blue's one of the colors you taught Lily about. Red and blue are her favorites."

Mumbling "Red," the girl tugged out the front of her own shirt, just before she raised both arms and hugged Coop around his neck.

Happily stunned, he blew a juicy kiss against the

child's ear. She made a noise that could have been a giggle and batted a hand over her ear.

"Oh, Coop, those are more words than she's ever attempted. This is more animation than she's ever shown at one time. I said before that you're good for her. I can't…I'm not denying that. It's me. It's us. Are *we* good for each other?" she exclaimed. "I can't help worrying. It's all so confusing."

"It doesn't have to be." Smiling, Coop stood and waltzed his soon-to-be daughter in a circle. "What I'm asking for is another chance. This is no place to talk. I'll wait here with Lily if you'll hunt up the driver of your bus. I assume you have suitcases. Come with me to the Triple D and we'll work everything out."

"You're a hard man to refuse. Okay. I'll go with you so we can talk more. But there's someone I need to say goodbye to. I met a really nice lady on the bus. A grandmother who's headed to San Antonio to take care of a special-needs grandson because the boy's dad is deployed overseas. Do you mind if I go talk to her first? I want to tell her what happened with Lilybelle."

"By all means. Any friend of yours is a friend of mine, Willow."

She'd jumped up from the bench, but checked her forward motion. "That's good. I want friends. It's something I missed desperately at the ranch. Tate hated for me to go to town. He didn't like me talking to anyone. He thought I was plotting against him, plotting to leave him, I guess," she said with a shake of her head.

"It's a shame you had to put up with his antics for as long as you did," Coop said with feeling.

"Yes, but like my mother said, it was a choice I made, and I had to honor my decisions."

"Belle said that?" Coop snorted. "I'm disappointed in her. What was she thinking?"

"Probably that she stuck with my dad through thick and thin."

"Hmph. She left most of it up to you, Willow." He waved a dismissive hand. "Oh, it doesn't matter now. Go find your friend, and then the driver."

"Dad was a paraplegic for a long time, Cooper. That took its toll on Mom and me. These days I'm sure there are more agencies to help families in our situation. Or maybe not," she said with a shrug. "Okay, I'm going. But I don't want you to hate my mom. She's Lily's only grandmother. Someday I'd like her to get to know Lily-belle."

"I don't hate her. I won't begrudge her visiting, but I believe she steered you wrong about suffering through a bad marriage. Living with a tough situation is one thing. Abuse is different."

"Mom didn't know about that. I never told her."

"You kept too much bottled up, Willow." Coop twirled a strand of her hair around his index finger until she pulled away.

"In hindsight, yes," Willow admitted. "But like you said, that's in the past." She took a step in the direction of the depot. "Wait here. I'll be right back."

Coop watched her hurry off and pass through the glass doors leading into the attached restaurant. He saw her bend down and speak to an older woman. People had begun to wander out. Some lit cigarettes. Others came to stand beside the door of the bus.

The child had drifted off to sleep, her forehead tucked against Coop's neck. He swayed from side to side, moving out of the way as more travelers emerged from the restaurant.

Willow walked out soon after, matching her steps to those of a big man in a bus driver's uniform. "It's highly unusual to give passengers their luggage at a stop before their final destination," Coop heard him say to Willow.

"Sorry for the imposition," he said, joining them. "I missed connecting with her in Carrizo Springs."

The driver stared from one to the other. "He's not forcing you to go with him, is he?" he asked, eyes raking Willow.

"Oh, no. Not at all!"

"Huh. All right, then. Do you remember which bin your bags are in? And I'll need the claim checks."

Willow dug in the canvas bag she had slung over one shoulder. "Here they are. Just two. Mine is a standard black case. Pretty beat up. My daughter's is smaller. Brown plaid."

Taking out a key, the driver opened the compartment Willow indicated. "There," she said, pointing.

The driver set the bags on the concrete. Willow bent to collect them, but Coop swooped down and grabbed the larger one. "I'd take them both," he said, "but Miss Lily is out like a light."

"I can see that. I'm concerned about how long she'l sleep. She wouldn't eat or drink what I brought for he supper. I hope she doesn't get dehydrated since it's suc a sultry night." Willow aimed her words at Coop, but a the bus driver left she caught his sleeve and thanked him

"You're welcome. All aboard for San Antonio," the man shouted, plodding ahead to open the bus.

"Where are you parked?" Willow asked Coop.

"Across the street. In the next block."

They crossed, and he noticed how pinched Willow's face was. "It's approximately seventy miles to Hondo, then another ten or so out to the ranch. How do you feel about staying here tonight, so we can all get a good night's rest? I know of a nice motel with a country-style restaurant next door. They're open twenty-four hours if you want to buy Lily a glass of milk. Did you pack her favorite cup? I can register and then run next door and have her cup filled while you settle in the room."

"One room, Coop? I... We really haven't worked anything out."

"I'll see if they have a suite. But if they don't, I wish you'd believe I'm exhausted, and I can see you are, too. And we have Lily with us."

"Staying here tonight is fine, Cooper. I certainly can't imagine the three of us barging in on your brother and his wife after midnight. What would I say to him?"

"Don't worry about Sully." Coop opened the pickup doors. He tossed the suitcases into the backseats, then handed Willow in and eased Lilybelle onto her lap. "I'll deal with him. I've already set out my conditions for going home. I promise you, Willow, if he says one disparaging thing, or doesn't accept you, we will not stay at the Triple D. I'll get an appraisal and he can buy out my share. I won't ask for half, since he's carried the workload for a long time. But...Blythe told me Sully's developed high blood pressure. That's what killed our father," Coop said, sounding worried.

As he got in his side, she carefully buckled Lilybelle between them before putting on her own seat belt. The new booster seat was still back in her old pickup. "I will *not* let you split with him, Coop. As I said, I refuse to be the reason for a deeper rift between you and Sullivan."

"No, Willow. I want you in my life. It makes me mad all over again when I think of what he said—blaming you for me running off to the rodeo."

"Was he right? After all, I never tried to contact you." She stared at her hands as he started the engine. "I'm the one who let fear mess up our lives."

"Fear? What do you mean?"

"I tried to tell you how scared I was that you'd get bucked off or smashed against a chute. That you'd be hurt like my dad was."

"I told you bulls were way more dangerous. I'd ridden bucking horses since I was thirteen."

"You still don't get it, Coop. There was no difference in my mind. I had nightmares about a horse stomping the life out of you."

"Willow, for God's sake, why didn't you tell me?"

"I assumed you could see the toll my father's injury took on Mom and me. And I knew that if I made you give up a dream, eventually you'd resent me for it. That last time we did talk, I tried to articulate how I felt. You didn't get it or seem to care. You went to Mesquite. So, I gave up. By then Dad was having seizures and I needed to go home instead of staying in school. I told my study group that evening. Tate was there. He failed two classes and was retaking them. You know he was always after me to go out with him. But he never came around when you were there."

Coop ground the gears pulling out. "I told you before that I'd rather not talk about Tate. It's pointless." He tossed his Stetson in the backseat and ran his hand through his dark hair.

"You need to hear it all, Coop. I want to tell you how things happened. The next night some of my friends were going to a movie and asked me along. I knew I'd be gone in a week and I'd be back home taking care of Dad. Tate offered me a ride back to the dorm. He said the same six or so couples were planning an end-of-the-year party at a popular club the next night. I'd never been, so I agreed to go. I got tipsy. Well, more than tipsy, to tell you the truth. Tate took care of me."

Cooper broke in again, but Willow shushed him. "A month after I got home, Daddy died unexpectedly. I felt guilty for being angry about having to leave college. Yes, you sent flowers, but Tate was there and he helped us handle stuff. He was solicitous of me and Mom. I just felt...numb. Your brother brought me to tears at the reception after the service. He yelled at me, like I said. Tate heard it all. He took me outside and proposed right then and there. He sounded sincere, and he promised we could move away from Hondo. I didn't want to stay where I could run into you any time you came home from the circuit. I grabbed Tate's offer like a lifeline."

Willow rubbed her forehead, hardly noticing that Coop had pulled into the parking lot of a western-style motel. "Well, you know the rest," she said, gesturing with one hand, her eyes closed. "His feelings for me were superficial at best."

"I'd like this to be the very last time we discuss Tate. Or any of the Walkers. Well, maybe not Bart. The sheriff said he stole your ranch because he thinks there's oil. If he strikes it rich, I'll gladly help you hire a lawyer to sue him on Lily's behalf. Maybe even if the well comes up dry. The way he's treating you two is wrong."

"Coop, I can't swear I'll never mention Tate. He *was* Lily's father. It'll be her right to know that someday. Even if I have to whitewash his history, I don't want her only to hear about his bad side. If you can't handle hearing Tate's name now and then, we shouldn't take our relationship further. The biggest question is, are you liable to resent Lily down the road for being his child?"

"No! I swear to you I'd never do that." Coop reached across Lilybelle and took Willow's hands. "And we can talk about Tate if necessary." He sighed. "I know we can't change the past, but we can shape our future. Ours and Lily's. While I was at your ranch I realized I've always loved you. I'll be honest. There were times I didn't want to. But when I found you again, I couldn't deny wanting to be with you. I want to be a husband to you and be a real dad to Lily. Will you let me?"

Chapter Fourteen

Willow gazed at Coop for a long moment. "I think I should wait to make that decision until we get to the Triple D tomorrow and see what our reception is. If your brother objects to me being back in your life, I won't stay. I mean, the Triple D is where you belong, Coop. It's your birthright as much as Sullivan's."

"The Triple D is land and an empty house. You're the woman I love. The woman I want to spend the rest of my life with. Our getting married has to do with us. Nobody else, Sully has no say."

Willow wished she believed that, but something in her wasn't reassured.

Lily stirred on the seat between them, shifting her head to Coop's leg. For a second her eyelashes fluttered, her eyes opened. She saw him, then snuggled back.

"I want to be your wife," Willow murmured. "I'd like us to be a family more than anything I've ever wanted. And, you know, I don't regret that Bart Walker took the ranch. I was stuck in a rut there. I can't care if Sully approves of me or not. No, that's a lie...I do care, Coop. I hope for your sake he forgives what he thinks

I did. I love you like I've loved no one else. I've got to admit I have reservations, but I...yes, I'll marry you."

Coop's eyes glowed with pleasure. He already held Willow's hand, and because her daughter lay sprawled across his leg, all he could do was press several kisses into Willow's palm. "I want to give you a better kiss," he said. "And I will. But before the motel staff sends cops to investigate why we're parked in their lot and no one's come inside, I need to go book us a room. Do you still want a suite?"

Willow smiled. "No, but nothing's really changed. It's late. We're tired. Lily will share our room and maybe even our bed, so it's all about sleeping tonight."

"If they have a room with two queens, Lily can have a bed of her own. And at least I can fall asleep holding you in my arms. Tomorrow night, though, we'll—"

"Coop, this may be the second time around for me, but I'm obviously shier about discussing what goes on in the bedroom than you are."

Coop carefully lifted the groggy child and put her in Willow's arms. "You never used to be. And you didn't seem at all shy to me the other night when we made love on your living-room floor."

She cleared her throat. "I don't recall that we talked about having sex first. We just...acted on our urges. Our feelings. It happened because I love you."

"That's what I mean. Maybe sex can be awkward, but when the people involved love each other, it's natural. An expression of shared feelings."

"Wow, I never knew you could be so poetic," Willow teased.

"And I'm even better at showing than telling." With

that, Coop opened the door, left the cab and strode into the motel lobby.

He soon returned with a key card. "We're at the back. I'll drive around, park and turn the horses out in their corral."

"The motel has a corral?"

"That's how I know the place. It's not a chain. It's owned by an ex-rodeo couple. They cater to guys and gals on the circuit, or to cowboys passing through."

"You've traveled all over the state. This is all so new to me."

"Really? Where did you go on your honeymoon?"

Willow hesitated, and didn't respond until Coop had parked out by the stables and corral. "No honeymoon," she finally said. "Tate and his dad drove to Carrizo Springs and closed on the ranch after Tate and I visited a justice of the peace. His dad tried to talk him into an annulment. Tate refused, but just knowing that threw me off balance. But we were married, so I drove down in Tate's pickup the next day. Nothing about my wedding or my marriage was romantic."

"You can bank on us having a honeymoon. Even if we take Lily along and make it a nice vacation. I want us to have something memorable. With photos to pass down to Lily and any other kids we have." He frowned as he went around the pickup to help Willow out. "We didn't discuss that possibility. Do you want more children?"

Running a finger lightly over the buttons down the front of Cooper's shirt, Willow nodded. "I do want your children, Coop."

He clasped her by the shoulders, taking care not to

bump the sleeping girl she held. Nevertheless he managed a deep and searing kiss. "We're in room twelve," he said in a voice rough with desire. "You go on in. After I turn out the horses, shall I go next door and get her some milk? You never said if you packed her cup with the lid." He handed her the room card.

"Listen to us. We sound like an old married couple. Yes, I packed her cup. I'll get it. If she wakes up, milk should last her until morning. I hope they have pancakes for breakfast, which she loves."

"I'll pick up a menu while I'm at the restaurant. Or do you want to walk over there for dinner?"

"I'm not really hungry. Anyway, I have apples, cheese and a sandwich I made for the trip."

"Okay." Coop set all three bags inside the room dominated by a king-size bed. A shower was visible through an open door. The decor—in browns and rust, complete with a wagon-wheel light fixture overhead— gave it an aura of the old west. "King-size beds were all they had left." He turned back one side of the covers. "Put Lily down here. You get the middle and I'll crawl in on the far side." Coop backed toward the door. "Uh, I almost forgot her cup."

She nodded, dug around in her suitcase and gave him the cup.

"I told Sully to open up the home place for us, Willow. He and Blythe built a new house. I'm not sure which, if any, furnishings they took. It used to be nicely furnished, but if you don't like how it's decorated, we'll get different stuff. It'll be your home, Willow. I want you to be happy there."

Moved, she curved her hand around his cheek. "You're assuming Sullivan will welcome me."

Turning his head, Coop again kissed her palm. "I wish you'd stop worrying. As kids Sully and I fought like, well, brothers." Coop hesitated a moment. "He had to grow up fast when Mom died. Being the oldest, he took over the accounting that she'd handled. When Dad died, running the ranch fell on Sully's shoulders because I was still in school. Until I spent time with your cattle in the past few weeks—vaccinating, branding and then negotiating prices for them—I never gave Sully enough credit. I can see I acted like the spoiled younger brother. I suppose he deserves an apology from me. Our parents were decent and loving folks, and I believe Sully and I can be like them. We can forge a truce. Blythe was sure of it."

"I hope so. I really do." Willow watched Coop step out of the door. As it shut she battled a sinking feeling. Was Coop being too much of an optimist? His brother had run the Triple D alone for seven or eight years now. It stood to reason that he'd be used to control. Sighing, she ate two apple slices and a piece of cheese, but she really wasn't hungry.

Lily woke up when Willow tried to put her in her pajamas. She fussed and not even her rabbit appeased her, so Willow decided to let her sleep in the shorts and shirt she had on. But she worried that Lily's sobs might wake people in the adjoining room. Theirs was on the end so they only shared one wall. Willow wished she had her rocker, but had to make do with an overstuffed leather chair.

Coop came in about the time Lily's cries reached a

crescendo. "Hey, hey, sweetie, what's the matter?" He lifted her from Willow's lap and offered her the cold milk. She took it and drank, barely sniffling between gulps, her forehead against Coop's cheek.

"She was really thirsty," Willow remarked.

The little girl took a final swig and handed the cup to her mother.

"Usually she drops her cup on the floor." Willow offered Lily some cheese, but the girl ducked her head in refusal.

Instead, Lily patted Coop's shoulder. "Blue," she said, clearly and distinctly as she kept patting his shirt.

"I guess Blue is going to be my new name. That's okay. When I think about it, I have more blue shirts than any other color." He jiggled the girl and smiled at her. "Blue, it is, Miss Lily."

"The fact that she's getting the color right repeatedly is very significant. I should've tried crayons a second time. The counselor told me to read the same book over and over and to show her the pictures so the images would stick in her mind." She shook her head. "The blocks you bought were another great idea. She loved stacking them according to size and color, but I had to leave them behind. The most progress she's made has been since you entered our lives, Coop. So…now I have doubts about whether keeping her at home with me was the best thing for her. Maybe it held her back."

Coop waited as she washed Lily's face and hands. He let her tuck the girl under the sheet before he spoke. "I'm no authority on kids, but it *can't* be a detriment for a young child to stay with her mother. To stay in familiar surroundings. If Blythe hasn't found a good day school for autistic kids, we'll research until we locate one so she can come home every night. We'll get her more blocks and whatever else she needs."

Willow dashed a hand across her eyes. "You keep making me cry. Thank you for everything, Coop. I love her so much." Willow smoothed back the girl's curls as her eyelids drifted closed.

Tugging Willow up and into his arms, then wrapping her in a tight hug, Coop said, "Thank you for allowing me to be part of her life. If there are answers to be had, we'll find them. Honey, you're running on empty. I'll sit with her until she's asleep if you'd like to go shower. It might help you sleep."

"I'll wait and shower in the morning. Trust me, I'll sleep no problem." Willow tucked her head under Coop's chin and pressed a kiss to his throat. "I feel safe with you here," she murmured.

"Don't kiss me again like that or I won't vouch for how safe you'll be," he teased as he lifted her chin with a finger and brushed a kiss on the tip of her nose. "Get ready for bed. I'll take off my shirt and boots and sleep in my jeans—in deference to our little bedmate."

"I sleep in a pair of old shorts and a T-shirt. Will it be an affront to your sensibilities if I change into them for the rest of the night?"

"Nope, but I should warn you I usually sleep in the raw. Ever since we got back together the other night, I felt it should be our de rigueur attire." Coop waggled his eyebrows.

Willow turned from pulling her nightclothes out of her suitcase and laughed. "There you go again, using ten-dollar words, cowboy. I say, keep on dreaming. All things risqué fall by the wayside with parenthood." She smiled at him and headed for the adjacent bath.

"Isn't that why bedroom doors have locks? There are ways," he called after her, although he barely raised his voice. "Otherwise, everyone would be an only child."

She poked her head out of the room. "I'll leave it up to you to figure it out, Coop. But tonight I'm tired, I'll be asleep as soon as my head hits the pillow."

"I wasn't talking about tonight. For once, I'm going to plan ahead. You can count on that."

She smiled to herself. And it'd been so long since she could count on anyone except herself, the burdens weighing her down suddenly felt lighter.

Coop was snoring softly by the time Willow had sponged off the grime of travel and emerged again, feeling better. She took a minute to admire the bare torso of the man with whom she'd be sharing a bed. Luck had finally fallen on her side. She snapped off the bedside lamp and crawled between the two sleeping bodies—the two most important people in her life. In spite of telling Coop how quickly she'd fall asleep, Willow lay awake worrying, wondering if her luck would hold after they reached the Triple D. Sullivan Drummond remained a wild card. As much as she loved Coop, she couldn't—wouldn't—come between the brothers.

RAYS OF SUNLIGHT dancing across the bed woke her the next morning. Some time during the night, Coop had draped an arm around her. Lily, totally relaxed as only a child could be, took up more than her third of the bed.

Used to rising at dawn to start on ranch chores,

Willow did her best to not move a muscle. Waking up in Coop's arms was as close to perfect as any fantasy she'd ever had.

But she wasn't the only one used to getting up early. "Good morning, sweetheart," a husky voice growled near her ear. Coop released her and stretched his arms. "At the risk of sounding 'poetic' again…your hair looks like ropes of spun gold in the morning sun. Do you always braid your hair at night? There's so much I don't know about you, Willow—so many facts and details. I can't wait to learn it all." Coop brushed a thumb over the end of one of her braids.

Pleasure clogged Willow's throat. She turned in his arms, pulling her hair from his loose grasp. Laying her right hand on his whiskery cheek, she kissed him, pouring every bit of love she could muster into that kiss.

"Mmm…I could handle being greeted like this *every* morning."

The moment ended because Lily sat up, rubbed her eyes and looped one arm around her plush rabbit. Looking around, the child seemed to take in all her surroundings, then climbed over her mother, patted Cooper's bare chest and, more clearly than she'd ever spoken, said, "No boo."

Coop laughed and tossed her in the air. "No *blue*. You're absolutely right, Lily B. I am not wearing a blue shirt today. Give me a second. You stay here with your mom. I'll shower and put on another blue shirt, just for you."

He scooted out of bed and grabbed his duffel.

Willow hugged the girl. "Two words. You put *two words* together. That makes Mama so happy."

Her tears of joy fell unabashedly when, for the very first time, her daughter touched her face and said, "Mama."

"Oh, yes, yes, yes. I'm Mama, and you're Lilybelle. This is Mr. Rabbit. Shall we find you a clean shirt to wear?" Willow marveled at her daughter and let her happy tears continue to flow.

"Red," the girl said, tugging on the shirt she'd worn to bed. It was as if words that had been stored in her head suddenly began to stream out.

"Yes. Let's keep this floodgate of words open, honeybee."

Glancing around again, Lily stretched out an arm in the direction of what would've been their kitchen at home. "Eat," she said.

Willow smothered her in hugs. "Clothes first, then I'll take a fast shower, then we'll go eat. Would you like pancakes?"

Lily rocked a bit and it seemed to Willow that she nodded. All of this was such a giant leap forward and filled Willow's heart with joy. Maybe leaving the ranch was good for all of them. Except that one man held the power to ruin everything. *Sullivan Drummond.*

Coop came out of the bathroom as Willow pulled a clean red T-shirt over Lily's curls. She wore it with yellow shorts that had red flowered pockets. "Your turn," Coop said, bending to stuff his rolled-up dirty clothes in a zippered pocket of his duffel. "I heard you say pancakes. If she'll let me, I'll put on her shoes and socks while you shower. When you're finished, I'll stow our bags in the truck, check out and meet you at the restaurant."

"You do plan ahead." Willow grinned. "I wish you'd heard Lily say more words this morning," she added wistfully. "New ones. New words. *Mama* was one, and you can't believe how…wonderful it sounded." Willow sniffed and had to grab a tissue.

"Hey, that's fantastic! And it's only the beginning. Are you okay?" he asked, raising Willow's face as he studied her anxious blue eyes.

"The counselor told me some nonverbal autistic children stay locked in their own worlds. I was afraid that was going to be Lily. Oh, I wish this morning could go on forever. I won't lie, Coop, I'm nervous about what might be waiting for us at the Triple D. Even if your brother didn't think I was bad for you, what can I actually bring to our marriage?"

"What do you mean? You bring yourself!"

"Right. Your sister-in-law is a doctor. I'm a college dropout."

"So what? Big deal." Coop set his bag and Lily's by the door. He sat the child on the bed and knelt with her socks in his hand. "I don't seem to be able to relieve your concerns. Apparently nothing but going there and getting the meeting over with will ease your mind. By ten o'clock your worries will be a thing of the past."

Willow wished she didn't worry so much, but life had brought her too many jolts, and she couldn't help expecting the worst. Yet she jumped in the shower and did her best to let the hot water wash her cares away. She hadn't packed any cosmetics, but she brushed her hair into a shine. She chose to wear her only pair of capris, white, which she teamed with a bright yellow T-shirt. While it was far from new, the color lifted her spirits.

"You look fantastic," Coop said. He punctuated his enthusiasm with a kiss that kicked Willow's heart into overdrive. "Meet you in ten minutes at the restaurant. Try to get a seat by the window on the back. It looks out on an area where there are rabbits. I think Lily will like that."

Taking her daughter's hand, Willow left the room and walked out into the heat of the morning sun.

Lily did love the rabbits. They had trouble getting her to eat, but all of them finally enjoyed hearty breakfasts and were on the road by half past eight.

With each mile they traveled Coop could see Willow's eyes grow cloudier. He wished he could convince her that it truly didn't matter to him how Sully reacted or whether he made them welcome at the Triple D. Willow and Lily were his destiny, come what may.

A few miles from Hondo, Coop cast a glance at Willow. "Have you thought any more about taking classes to finish up your teaching degree?"

She whipped her head around. "I've been out of the habit of studying for five years. I...don't know if I could get back into the swing of it. There's Lily, too. To say nothing of tuition costs. You mentioned loans, but they have to be paid back."

"What about online classes to start? I met a few guys on the circuit who'd also dropped out of college. They set up laptops in their motor homes and caught up on some of their courses. If it interests you, we can look into it. See a college counselor. Ask about loans. Jus for the record, I don't give a damn if you get a degree or not. But I sense it's something that bothers you."

"It does. I was so close. And ever since Lilybelle was diagnosed, I thought if I had my teaching degree it wouldn't be hard to pick up extra credits in special education. I'd be able to help her and other kids like her."

"If that's what you want, we'll set that goal right now."

Willow's eyes glowed with an inner brightness for the first time during their drive. Coop shoved a CD into the player and they listened to Reba's song "A Little Want To." The words expressed their thoughts perfectly....

Willow tensed up again when they'd skirted Hondo. Coop swung his pickup out and turned down the poplar-lined gravel drive that marked the entrance to the Triple D. The home place, where Coop had been raised sat straight ahead. But, he saw a new mailbox at the end of a new road that had been cut through the land. Smaller trees had been planted along both sides. Assuming it led to Sully's new house, Coop made a sharp turn and glanced in his side mirrors. "Hope I didn't toss Legend and Rusty around too much."

As he parked in the circular drive, he whistled through his teeth. "Some digs," he said. "Looks like a place out of *Architectural Digest.*"

The house sat on a hill and overlooked a valley of green dotted with white-faced cattle. The pristine rail fence was a far cry from the wire Coop had strung on metal posts at Willow's ranch. Where her house had a porch, this home had a *porch,* one that wrapped around the cedar-sided house with peaks of glass. He saw an arrangement of wicker outdoor furniture, grouped around a fire pit. "Son of a...gun," he said. "And Sully tried to make me think he was working his butt off to make ends meet."

"Coop, are we going to sit here all morning?" Willow asked. "Someone's come out on the porch."

He reined in his roaming eyes and cracked open his door. "That's Blythe and Gray. Their son."

Climbing out, Coop rushed around the cab and opened Willow's door. Her fingers weren't steady. He ended up unbuckling her seat belt and Lily's.

Blythe and her son rushed down the stone steps. "You did come! Couldn't you have called again, Cooper? We've been on pins and needles ever since you phoned yesterday to say you were going to get Willow off the bus."

Coop noticed that his brother was slower to come out of the house.

Sully's hands were tucked in his front jeans' pockets, and his face revealed nothing as he descended the steps.

Blythe hugged Coop, then Willow, who held one of Lily's hands. The girl clutched her ever-present rabbit in the other.

The brothers maintained a wary eye contact before Sullivan stood before Coop at last. Freeing his right hand, Sully gave his brother's shoulder a friendly slap. "Welcome home, Coop. It's about time." Then he turned his attention to Willow. "If you're the reason thi hardheaded so-and-so has finally come home where h belongs, I...we owe you," Sully said, placing one han on his wife's shoulder while extending the other toward Willow.

"I, ah, Coop decided all on his own."

Blythe bent at the waist. "And I'm assuming this is Lilybelle." She smiled at the child, who now clung tightly to her mother's leg. "This is our son, Gray. Honey, do you have a gift for your cousin? Well, soon-to-be cousin," she said, shooting Willow another wide smile.

The thin boy with big eyes and a shock of unruly dark hair edged forward. A foot from Lily, he held out a toy. A rainbow-colored pony with a pale silvery mane and tail that looked a lot like the one she'd colored. "For you," Gray mumbled. "Uncle Coop loves horses. He's gonna raise them on the Triple D."

Willow held her breath as all eyes shifted to her daughter. Surprisingly, Lily accepted the toy and bestowed a brief smile on her benefactor. "Po…ny," she said clearly.

The two women beamed at the kids. Willow mostly, because Sully and Blythe couldn't know what a huge step this was for Lily. Not only to accept an offering from a stranger, but to call it by its name. And a shy smile from a girl deficient in facial expression was a rare gift in itself. Willow blinked rapidly to keep tears at bay.

Coop focused on his nephew. "I don't know if I'm going to raise horses on the Triple D, Gray. We'll have to see. It's true I used to run a herd here, though."

As if on cue, the horses in Coop's trailer whinned. An answering whinny came from a fenced area across the lane. Swinging around, Coop saw a number of horses trotting along the enclosure. Shock rippled through him. "Sully, those look like part of the herd I sold after Dad died."

"When you sold them, refused to come home and later took off for the rodeo in a huff, you mean?" his brother asked mildly.

Blythe jabbed Sully in the ribs. "We said we wouldn't mention the past."

Sully tugged on one ear in a gesture Willow found endearingly reminiscent of Coop. "I bought them back," the older brother admitted. "I never believed you'd stay away from the Triple D forever. Although, after you quit the rodeo last year and then didn't come home, I have to say I began to have doubts."

Stuttering out words of gratitude that were trapped in his throat, Coop crossed the short space and gave his brother an awkward hug. He stepped back, picked up Lily and her toys, then slid his other arm around Willow's waist. "I'm home for good if you'll welcome my family. We haven't tied the knot yet, but Willow's agreed to marry me. Sooner rather than later, I hope. Lily has special needs that'll take priority with both of us. But I plan on working hard to support them," he vowed, smiling into Willow's eyes.

Sully exchanged a loving glance with Blythe before stepping forward. "Willow," he said, "you probably know that hotheadedness runs in the Drummond family. However, that's no excuse for the things I said to you at a rough time in your life. I hope you'll forgive me. I, of all people, should've known how shaky people feel when they've lost a loved one. I'm really sorry."

Willow bit her upper lip. "You're forgiven," she said. "I love Cooper." She edged closer to him, but then her voice failed her.

Nodding, Sully let his gaze rest momentarily on the other five members of their group. "Four of us are already Drummonds, and two soon will be. Coop, I happen to have an attorney on retainer. Since Dad died, I've had trouble calling the ranch the Triple D. What would you say to legally changing the ranch name and logo? We could just go back to calling it Drummond Ranch, if you like that idea, Cooper."

Coop's arm tightened around Willow. "You're asking my opinion and not giving me an order?"

"Blythe constantly reminds me that I'm not Dad. We're equal here, Cooper," Sully said, sounding fervent and a little humble.

Coop squared his shoulders. "I'd say it sounds good—and it'll still work when one or both of us add to our families," he said, slanting a wink toward the women.

He dropped his hand after a last small squeeze of Willow's waist and set Lily down by Gray. The brothers took off to inspect their two herds, cattle on one side of the road, horses on the other.

"That was a nice gesture," Willow murmured to Blythe. "I worried a lot about coming here with Coop. I made up my mind that, no matter what, I'd never come between Coop and his brother."

Blythe linked arms with Willow. "I'm so glad it didn't come to that. While they're off doing what Drummond men do, why don't you and I go inside and check the calendar for an end-of-summer wedding date? The home place, which now belongs to you and Cooper, has the perfect bridal staircase. You know their parents, Matt and Lily, were married there? So were Sully and I. Or if you'd rather book a church, we can do that," Blythe said as they walked through the door.

"The family house would be lovely, if it's okay with Coop. Thank you and Sullivan for making me and Lilybelle feel welcome. For making us feel like family," she said with a catch in her voice.

"You *are* family," Blythe insisted staunchly. "Coop said you named Lily after his mother. That's special, Willow. Oh, I promised him I'd research schools that teach language skills and cognitive development." Blythe pulled a packet of brochures from a credenza drawer and handed them to Willow. "You can evaluate the facilities after you get settled, and choose the one you like best for Lily. The program I'm most partial to is housed in the private school Gray attends. That way he'd be there as her older cousin, to look out for Lily."

The men walked into the house in time for Coop to hear his sister-in-law's suggestion. Sliding both arms around Willow, Coop brushed his cheek over her. "How does that sound to you, Willow? Hey, did Willow tell you she might go back to school herself, to finish her teaching degree? She could end up teaching Gray or Lily."

Blythe and Sully immediately congratulated her and offered her their support.

"This all seems too good to be true," Willow murmured as she clutched the brochures. "A day ago I w made homeless by my former father-in-law. Life was completely uncertain. Now I'm standing here in the middle of my new extended family. A real *family*," she whispered, reaching up to frame Cooper's other cheek. "I can't tell you how deeply that touches me."

"Uh, speaking of extended family—there's other news you may not have heard," Sully said. "Bart Walker sold the Bar W to Jud Rayburn. 'Course Bart knew I'd jump at a chance to buy land bordering our pastures. But he never would've sold it to me."

"Interesting," Coop returned, tightening his hold on Willow. "The sheriff in Carrizo Springs said Bart stole Willow's ranch because he expected to strike oil. But… drilling on the neighboring ranch went sour. It seems Bart may have screwed himself all around. Willow, are you okay with that? He *is* Lily's grandpa. But we could try, for Lily's sake, to sue his socks off."

Willow waved her free hand. "He'd have to change a whole lot for me ever to welcome him into Lily's life. If you're leaving it up to me, I say let him keep the ranch down south. Lilybelle and I are leaving our entire past behind, Coop. Soon we won't be Walkers. Lily and I are going to be the best Drummonds we can be."

"You're both perfect as you are," Coop said.

The others circled around Willow, hugging her, and suddenly Sully drew attention to the fact that Gray and Lily had gone to the porch, where his son was showing Lily how to snap together big, colorful plastic blocks.

"Would you look at that?" Coop said with feeling. "Our girl has made her first friend." He trailed a light and up Willow's back and murmured, "The road to getting here has been a long and winding one, but we're all home at last."

Tilting her head until it touched Coop's shoulder, Willow nodded, but her heart was too full to speak.

* * * * *

HEART & HOME

Harlequin®

American ★ Romance®

ou can find more information on upcoming Harlequin®
les, free excerpts and more at www.Harlequin.com.   HARCNM0512

REQUEST YOUR FREE BOOKS!
2 FREE NOVELS PLUS 2 FREE GIFTS!

♦ Harlequin®

American ★ Romance®

LOVE, HOME & HAPPINESS

YES! Please send me 2 FREE Harlequin® American Romance® novels and my 2 FREE gifts (gifts are worth about $10). After receiving them, if I don't wish to receive any more books, I can return the shipping statement marked "cancel." If I don't cancel, I will receive 4 brand-new novels every month and be billed just $4.49 per book in the U.S. or $5.24 per book in Canada. That's a saving of at least 14% off the cover price! It's quite a bargain! Shipping and handling is just 50¢ per book in the U.S. and 75¢ per book in Canada.* I understand that accepting the 2 free books and gifts places me under no obligation to buy anything. I can always return a shipment and cancel at any time. Even if I never buy another book, the two free books and gifts are mine to keep forever.

154/354 HDN FEP2

Name	(PLEASE PRINT)

Address		Apt. #

City	State/Prov.	Zip/Postal Code

Signature (if under 18, a parent or guardian must sign)

Mail to the **Reader Service:**
IN U.S.A.: P.O. Box 1867, Buffalo, NY 14240-1867
IN CANADA: P.O. Box 609, Fort Erie, Ontario L2A 5X3

Not valid for current subscribers to Harlequin American Romance books.

Want to try two free books from another line?
Call 1-800-873-8635 or visit www.ReaderService.com.

* Terms and prices subject to change without notice. Prices do not include applicable taxes. Sales tax applicable in N.Y. Canadian residents will be charged applicable taxes. Offer not valid in Quebec. This offer is limited to one order per household. All orders subject to credit approval. Credit or debit balances in a customer's account(s) may be offset by any other outstanding balance owed by or to the customer. Please allow 4 to 6 weeks for delivery. Offer available while quantities last.

SPECIAL EDITION

Life, Love and Family

USA TODAY bestselling author

Marie Ferrarella

enchants readers in

ONCE UPON A MATCHMAKER

Micah Muldare's aunt is worried that her nephew is going to wind up alone in his old age...but this matchmaking mama has just the thing! When Micah finds himself accused of theft, defense lawyer Tracy Ryan agrees to help him as a favor to his aunt, but soon finds herself drawn to more than just his case. Will Micah open up his heart and realize Tracy is his match?

Available June 2012

Saddle up with Harlequin® series books this summer and find a cowboy for every mood!

Available wherever books are sold.

www.Harlequin.com

HSE65674

A grim discovery is about to change everything for Detective Layne Sullivan—including how she interacts with her boss!

Read on for an exciting excerpt of the upcoming book UNRAVELING THE PAST by Beth Andrews....

SOMETHING WAS UP—otherwise why would Chief Ross Taylor summon her back out? As Detective Layne Sullivan walked over, she grudgingly admitted he was doing well. But that didn't change the fact that the Chief position should have been hers.

Taylor turned as she approached. "Detective Sullivan, we have a situation."

"What's the problem?"

He aimed his flashlight at the ground. The beam illuminated a dirt-encrusted skull.

"Definitely a problem." And not something she'd expected. Not here. "How'd you see it?"

"Jess stumbled upon it looking for her phone."

Layne looked to where his niece huddled on a log. "I'l contact the forensics lab."

"Already have a team on the way. I've also called in unit to search for the rest of the remains."

So he'd started the ball rolling. Then, she'd assume command while he took Jess home. "I have this under control

Though it was late, he was clean shaven and neat, his fl stomach a testament to his refusal to indulge in doughnu His dark blond hair was clipped at the sides, the top lo enough to curl.

The female part of Layne admitted he was attractive.

The cop in her resented the hell out of him for it.

"You get a lot of missing-persons cases here?" he ask

"People don't go missing from Mystic Point." Although plenty of them left. "But we have our share of crime."

"I'll take the lead on this one."

Bad enough he'd come to *her* town and taken the position she was meant to have, now he wanted to mess with *how* she did her job? "Why? I'm the only detective on third shift and your second in command."

"Careful, Detective, or you might overstep."

But she'd never played it safe.

"I don't think it's overstepping to clear the air. You have something against me?"

"I assign cases based on experience and expertise. You don't have to like how I do that, but if you need to question every decision, perhaps you'd be happier somewhere else."

"Are you threatening my job?"

He moved so close she could feel the warmth from his body. "I'm not threatening anything." His breath caressed her cheek. "I'm giving you the choice of what happens next."

What will Layne choose? Find out in
UNRAVELING THE PAST by Beth Andrews,
available June 2012 from Harlequin® Superromance®.

And be sure to look for the other two books
in Beth's THE TRUTH ABOUT THE SULLIVANS *series*
available in August and October 2012.

Harlequin Romance

A touching new duet from fan-favorite author

SUSAN MEIER

First Time DADS!

When millionaire CEO Max Montgomery spots
Kate Hunter-Montgomery—the wife he's never forgotten—
back in town with a daughter who looks just like him, he's
determined to win her back. But can this savvy business tycoon
convince Kate to trust him a second time with her heart?

Find out this June in

THE TYCOON'S SECRET DAUGHTER

And look for book 2 coming this August!

NANNY FOR THE MILLIONAIRE'S TWINS

Saddle up with Harlequin® series books this summer
and find a cowboy for every mood!